Today Libby said I'm not her best friend anymore. "You're not enough of a tomboy. You're turning into a real girly girl."

"I am not! I don't play with dolls," I said.

"What do you mean? You have around ten dolls at home," Libby said. "At *least*."

I felt really bad. Libby's been my best friend since I was four. And it isn't even like I changed that much. It's more that *she* changed. Maybe Libby will change again, not back to the old way, but to some different thing where she won't care so much about this stuff. If she doesn't, I don't know what I'll do. I guess I won't have a best friend anymore.

Other Bullseye Books you will enjoy

Confessions of an Only Child by Norma Klein
Scruffy by Jack Stoneley
The Trouble with Thirteen by Betty Miles
Skinnybones by Barbara Park

TOMBOY

TOMBOY

Norma Klein

BULLSEYE BOOKS · ALFRED A. KNOPF
New York

DR. M. JERRY WEISS, Distinguished Service Professor of Communications at Jersey City State College, is the educational consultant for Bullseye Books. A past chair of the International Reading Association President's Advisory Committee on Intellectual Freedom, he travels frequently to give workshops on the use of trade books in schools.

Library of Congress Catalog Card Number: 78-4337
ISBN: 0-394-82044-4 (pbk.)
RL: 4.3
First Bullseye edition: June 1989

Manufactured in the United States of America
0 1 2 3 4 5 6 7 8 9

To Betty

1

"This key better work," I said, "or we're in big trouble."

"Why shouldn't it?" Jimmy asked.

"Well, I never used it before—for coming home from school, I mean." I kept jiggling it around because Dad always says the bottom lock is the hardest one to do. Once you get that one, the top one is easy. "This is the first year I've had my own key," I said.

"I've had one since I was seven."

"Really?"

"Yeah. My parents work so I had to because nobody was there some of the time."

That made me feel sort of babyish, the same way I feel about Mom and Dad not letting me go to school alone till last year when I was in fourth grade. It's more Dad than Mom. He was brought up in the country and he says New York traffic makes him nervous. Mom grew up in New York so I guess she's more used to it.

"Maybe I'll have to ask the doorman," I said. I hoped I wouldn't have to because then Mom and Dad might decide I was too young to have my own key.

"Here, let me try it," Jimmy said. He wiggled the key around and all of a sudden it turned in the lock. "That was *easy,*" he said.

"*I* was wiggling it—I wonder what you did different." I took the key case from him and did the other lock.

The house was dark. That usually means Dad and Brendan are out shopping or something. I still don't like it that much, coming home when no one's there, but Mom said I just have to get used to it. When I was little, Mom was almost always there, or Inez, this lady who came to clean. But everything changed this year because Dad got laid off his job, meaning he doesn't have one anymore so we don't have as much money as we used to. Luckily, Mom finished law school and she has a job, but I guess it's not enough. That's what my parents talk about a lot these days, money and not having it and everybody in our family having to get used to things being not the same as they were. Of course, Brendan's only ten months old so he doesn't even remember *what* things used to be like. He's my baby brother and I'm getting to like him, sort of. I still say it wasn't so bad being an only child, but I guess I won't ever be one again. Well, at least I was one for almost ten years. It might sound like a funny coincidence to you but Brendan was born right on my best friend Libby's birthday. I remember she got sort of mad because she was having her tenth birthday party at school when Dad called up. All of a sudden everyone began talking about Brendan and not about it being her birthday. She got over it, though. She usually does.

Jimmy looked around my room. "Hey, neat!" he said. "You have the U.S.S. Enterprise Playset. I'm going to ask Dad for that for Christmas."

This year it seems like everyone at school is crazy about Star Trek. All everybody wants for Christmas is Star Trek stuff, Star Trek dolls and phasers and books.

"Do you watch it every night?" I asked.

"Yeah . . . I've seen every episode around three times."

"Me too. Only I missed some over the summer because we don't have a TV on Fire Island."

We played with the Enterprise for a while. Jimmy worked Captain Kirk and Dr. McCoy and I worked Spock and Lieutenant Uhura. One strange thing is my mother can't *stand* Star Trek. She thinks I'm crazy to keep watching it when I've already seen all the episodes. She doesn't like me to watch TV either. Once she even said she was going to throw our TV set out! She can get pretty wild at times. Then she made this rule that I could only watch one hour a day and two on weekends. She says if I sit glued to the TV all day, like on Saturday morning, I'll turn into a mindless blob. That's just dumb! I'm glad Dad, at least, understands. He says he loved science fiction when he was my age. He doesn't think it's crazy at all.

"Want to see my microphone?" I said.

"Is it a toy one?"

"No, it's real. I got it from my uncle. He works for some TV station." I went and got it out of the closet. I really love my microphone. In fact, I think you could say in some ways it's my favorite toy. What I like to do is pretend I'm a TV announcer and go around interviewing people.

I plugged it in and said, "Okay, folks. . . . Today we have with us Jimmy Sherrill, pupil at the New Lincoln School. We're very happy to have you with us today, Jimmy." I put the microphone down. "Let's pretend it's real, like a real interview, okay?"

"Okay," he said, smiling.

I sat cross-legged in front of him and said in my interviewing voice, which I think makes me sound much older, "Jimmy, I hear you're in fifth grade this year. How do you like it, compared to last year?"

"It's pretty good."

"I hear that you and some other kids who used to be in your class were put in with some younger kids."

"Yeah, we were." He cleared his throat and

looked a little nervous, like it was a real interview.

"How do you like the new kids in your class this year?"

"Oh, they're pretty good . . . except this one kind of weird one named Antonia Henderson."

That's me. Usually people call me Toe or Ant. I used to like that, but now I'd rather have my real name back. "What's so weird about her?" I said indignantly. I kind of forgot it was supposed to be an interview.

"Well, she has this idea that she's a TV interviewer. She really believes it."

"That doesn't sound so weird to me. . . . *I've* heard Antonia Henderson is terrific, one of the smartest kids in her class."

"She's pretty good. . . . She has this mustache, though, which is kind of peculiar."

"She *does*?"

"Yeah . . . I never saw one on a girl before."

Suddenly I put the microphone down. "I do *not* have a mustache," I said.

"Well, just kind of," Jimmy said. "It just *looks* like one."

I got up and went to look in the mirror. It was true, but I never even noticed it before.

"Hey, that microphone is great," Jimmy said, lifting it up. "Can I interview you?"

"Do you know how?"

"Well, I can just ask you questions like you were doing to me." He lifted the microphone up. "In a minute we'll present Ms. Antonia Henderson, world-famous fifth-grade student, but now, a word from our sponsor: Gloper's Peanut Butter." He began horsing around, pretending to do a commercial. "So, if you want the gloppiest, yuckiest, most disgusting peanut butter you ever tasted, try Gloper's."

"Jimmy, listen, you can't interview me."

"Why not?"

"Because I have to walk these dogs." I didn't realize it was past five.

"What dogs?"

"It's my job. I do it every day." Actually I just got the job this year. Mom and Dad said two dogs a day is enough, but I wish I could do more. They said otherwise I'd spend all my time dog walking and wouldn't ever get homework done or anything. "You can come with me," I said. "One of them's right in this building."

"Okay," Jimmy said.

2

Mrs. Shorr is this grandmother who lives on our floor. She didn't even want Hortense, the basset hound she has now, but her daughter, who's really grown up and has children, couldn't keep her anymore because she had a child who was allergic to dog hair. So Mrs. Shorr said she'd take her. Hortense is really old—almost as old as one of our dogs. We have two, Elvira, this little Yorkshire terrier Mom had from before she was married, and William, who's a German short-haired pointer. He's pretty young. Dad usually takes the dogs with him when he takes Brendan out for a walk. I knew they weren't home because when they are, they come sniffing and whining around the front door before you open it, even.

Mrs. Shorr was in, like she usually is. She smiled at us. I said, "This is Jimmy, Mrs. Shorr. He's a friend of mine from school."

"You may have a little trouble with Hortense today," Mrs. Shorr said, fastening on Hortense's muzzle. "She just hates the rain."

"You ought to get her a raincoat," Jimmy said.

"I suppose so. Well, take this umbrella and hold it over her as best you can."

Some dogs like rain, but not Hortense. It seems like she can even *smell* when it's raining because once, we get to the lobby, she begins walking really slowly, and she walks pretty slowly anyway. Then, when we got to the front door, she began pulling back on her leash. I had to kind of yank her out.

Walking Hortense is not so great in certain ways. First, there's the way she is about rain. When it snows, she sometimes gets salt between her toes or whatever that stuff is they sprinkle on sidewalks. All of a sudden she'll start hobbling and I have to kind of lug her home. She's pretty heavy. But the worse thing is she likes to eat garbage. That's why Mrs. Shorr has her wear a muzzle.

"Does she bite?" Jimmy said as we walked out in the rain. We both had slickers on so we didn't care about having to hold the umbrella over Hortense.

"Uh-uh. She eats all this junk, though."

"What kind of junk?"

"Oh, garbage and everything." I didn't want to tell him that she even eats woofies sometimes. That's what Mrs. Shorr calls b.m. When I walk Hortense, people always ask me about the muzzle. They can't believe a basset hound would be that ferocious. I guess it would be a good way to protect yourself, making people *think* you had a ferocious dog when you really didn't.

"I wish *we* could have a dog," Jimmy said, "but my parents think it's not fair to have one in the city."

"Dad takes William for a long run every day so he doesn't mind it so much," I said. "And Elvira is so old she doesn't even like to go out much."

Usually Mrs. Shorr asks me in for some cookies and milk after I walk Hortense, but this time, maybe because Jimmy was with me, she didn't. She pays me once a week, a quarter for each walk.

"You don't have to come with me for Freddie," I said. "He's down the block."

"Oh, I'll come," Jimmy said. "I don't have to be home till six. Who's Freddie?"

"He's a dachshund."

In some ways I don't like Freddie so much. He always barks at me. You'd think by now he'd know me since I've been walking him for a few months. Mrs. Bergson says he's neurotic. Like, he'll be lying under the stove eating this old bone and when I come over with the leash, he'll start growling, like he thought I wanted to *eat* this yucky old bone he's been chewing on for around a thousand years. Freddie has lots of sweaters and coats because the Bergsons say dachshunds are delicate. Only once you get his sweater on, he won't let you take it off when you come back upstairs so I just leave it on him.

"Aren't you going to ring?" Jimmy asked when we came to the Bergsons' front door.

"No, they don't come home until seven. That's why I have to walk him. They gave me their key."

"How come the radio's on?" Jimmy said.

You could hear music coming from inside the apartment. "That's to keep him company," I explained. It is slightly strange, but evidently Freddie hates to be alone and the Bergsons have to keep the radio going all day so he'll hear voices and think there's someone there. Even then Mr. Bergson says sometimes Freddie starts howling and all the neighbors hear him and think he's being beaten or something.

By the time we got Freddie down, the rain was letting up. "When I grow up, I think I'll be a dog trainer," I said, "or a TV announcer. What're you going to be?"

Jimmy thought a moment. "I guess I might be an astronaut," he said. "Or maybe just the kind of person who designs rockets and stuff like that."

"The kind that go to outer space?"

He nodded. "Maybe by then everything that happens in Star Trek will really happen."

"You mean there being other worlds?"

"Maybe."

We walked Freddie just to the corner and back. Mom says I can't go into the park after it gets dark. When I walk Freddie on weekends, like on Saturday if the Bergsons are away for the day, I take him into the park, but not on regular school days.

Jimmy didn't come upstairs with me because he said he had to go home. He lives about ten blocks from me. By the time I got upstairs, Dad was home. He was in the bathroom giving Brendan his bath.

You can put Brendan in a real bathtub now. Before, Dad used to do him in the sink, but now he can sit up and everything. He has these old bath toys that used to be mine, a chime ball and some rubber animals and a boat. He just sits there, hitting them and making these queer squeaking noises. Dad was sitting on the bathroom floor, reading the paper.

"Toe, you didn't double lock the door when you went out," he said.

"Oh, I'm sorry." I guess I had so much trouble getting it open, I forgot.

"Did the key work all right?"

I didn't want to tell him that Jimmy had opened the door. I just nodded and sat down next to him. "Dad?"

"Umm?" He was still looking at the paper.

"Do you mind that I have a mustache?"

He thought a minute. "I don't like it as much as your beard, but, as mustaches go, it's pretty fine."

"Dad, I mean it! Seriously."

"What mustache are you talking about?"

"These, like, hairs. . . . Jimmy said it looked like a mustache."

Dad looked at me closely. "I guess I never noticed."

"Neither did I."

"Honey, I think you look fine. What can I say?"

"That's just because I'm your daughter."

"Maybe. But, even trying to be objective, I'd say that anyone who says you have a mustache is being kind of mean."

"He didn't say it to be mean."

"What did he say it for?"

"I don't know."

"Maybe he has a crush on you. I remember when I used to like girls, I would kind of tease them about things."

"He doesn't," I said. "I know." I tried to imagine Dad as a little boy, but it was hard. I guess I tend to imagine him looking as he does now, but smaller.

"Don't worry about it, honey, it's not worth it. Why don't you get me a pair of Brendan's pajamas, okay? And a fresh Pamper?"

In the hall closet there are always around four boxes of Pampers. When Dad goes shopping, he has to get lots because Brendan uses them up so fast. Sometimes, even when you're in the middle of changing him, he goes again. I don't like changing him. It's all smelly.

"Well, this looks like a pretty clean baby, I'd say," Dad said, wrapping Brendan up in this big towel and laying him down on the bath mat. Brendan began wriggling around, cooing and making those noises babies make. "Now, I ask you," Dad said, sprinkling him with powder, "have you ever seen a cleaner baby than this? Tell me the truth, Toe."

"Sure, he looks pretty clean," I said.

It's funny the way grownups talk to babies. I mean, you'd think, what's the point? The baby can't understand anything, but it seems like grownups just do it anyway. I sat there, cross-legged, watching Dad get Brendan into his stretch suit. He wears those most of the time, at night, or in the day, except they're always getting wet so you have to keep changing him.

I don't think I'm jealous of Brendan the way they say sisters and brothers are. So he's a baby, so what? Big deal. But I am jealous of one thing— that he's with Dad all day. I wish I could've been when I was a baby. I wish Dad had been laid off *then* instead of now.

3

Today Libby said I'm not her best friend any-more. "You're not enough of a tomboy," she said.

"I am too," I said. We were at school, during lunchtime. The reason I found out about not being her best friend is I heard her talking with Florence Meyer and Ginny Rule about this club they were starting. I thought they were going to ask me too, but then they started whispering to-gether and Libby came over and said they wouldn't let me join. I never even said I *wanted* to join their dumb club!

"You don't care that much about sports," Libby said.

"I do too," I said. That's kind of a lie, really. The thing is, I'm just not that good at sports. Like if someone throws a ball at me, I usually drop it. And lots of times, right in the middle of a game, I don't pay attention. We'll be playing baseball and I'll start thinking about some other thing. I'll forget what I'm supposed to be doing. Mom says it's just that I'm absentminded, like someone who puts on socks that don't match.

Anyway, till this year Libby never cared that much about sports.

"You're turning into a real girly girl," she said.

Libby says there are two kinds of girls—tomboys and girly girls. Tomboys like sports and wear jeans all the time with flies in the front. Libby says if you just wear regular pants, the kind that pull on, that doesn't count. You have to wear the kind that boys wear. I guess if you wore dresses, that would be even worse, but none of the girls in our class do anymore. The only one who does is Gretchen, who has her leg in this brace and pants don't fit on over it.

"I don't play with dolls," I said. Actually, I do play with the dolls that came with my Star Trek Playset, but that's different. They're not like baby dolls so much.

"What do you mean? You have around ten dolls at home," Libby said. "At *least*."

"Well, so do you."

"We just keep them for Mattie," Libby said. "She's still a baby." Mattie is Libby's sister. She's around three.

"Well, we keep mine for Brendan, for when he gets bigger," I said.

"Boys don't like dolls, that isn't even *true*," Libby said.

"How do you know? You don't even have a brother," I said.

I went home feeling really bad. Libby's been my best friend since I was four. We used to visit each other all the time. And it isn't even like I changed that much. It's more that *she* changed. I can't help it if I'm not good at sports, can I?

That night I asked Mom if she would get me some new pants, the kind with flies.

"But your pants fit perfectly well," Mom said. "I even had to take up the hems. You can wear them for another year, at least."

"But then Libby'll think I'm a girly girl," I muttered.

"A what?" Mom said.

"She says if you don't wear pants with flies, just like a boy's, you're a girly girl."

Mom sighed. "Libby's brain must be giving way."

"It's for the Tomboy Club," I tried to explain. "Libby says I can't join. She says I'm not enough of a tomboy." I started feeling like I might cry.

Mom squeezed my shoulder. "Honey! That's just crazy! Anyway, there's no such *thing* as a tomboy."

"There is *too*!" I said, pulling away. "It's a real word."

"What is a tomboy?"

"It's a girl who acts like a boy."

"But don't you see, that's saying there's a certain way girls should act and a certain way boys should act. That's so old-fashioned! I'm surprised at Libby."

"It's *not*. And another thing is, you have to be good at sports."

"Since when is being good at sports acting like a boy?"

"It just *is*. Everyone knows that," I said.

Mom shook her head. "I think I'm getting a headache," she said. "I'm going to lie down."

I followed her into the living room where she lay down on the couch. "And I want to give away *all* my dolls," I said.

"Honey, let's forget all this nonsense, okay?"

"I'm too *big* for dolls," I said desperately. "We have around nine million dolls and they take up all this room."

"So weed out a few that are kind of old and we'll give those away."

"Why not give them *all* away?"

"Because they're nice dolls! I like them! *I'll* play with them."

I sighed. The thing is, I still do like some of my dolls. Maybe I can just hide them so when Libby visits me, if she ever does, she won't see them. I could put them in some special box in the back of the closet and maybe even put a lock on the box.

When Dad came home from his pottery class that he teaches downtown, I went into the kitchen to help him with dinner. "Dad, do you think there's such a thing as a tomboy?" I said.

Dad was feeding Brendan, who was wiggling around and messing with his food like he always does. I don't understand why he's so fat because all he does is mess around—he hardly seems to eat anything. "What was that, Toe? I'm sorry, I wasn't listening."

"What's a tomboy?" I said.

"A girl who acts like a boy," Dad said, giving Brendan a hard-boiled egg, chopped up in pieces.

"But Mom says there is no such *thing*! She says that's old-fashioned."

"Oh yeah . . . well, I guess looked at in a certain light, I see what she means."

"Dad, were you good at sports when you were little?"

"Not especially. Why?"

"Did you mind?"

Dad thought a minute. "Well, I had this friend, Billy, who was even worse than me. I guess that made it easier."

I went inside to look at my dolls and try to decide which ones to weed out. The trouble is, some of the old ones I still like. I can't exactly explain why. Like, I have this doll named Gabbigale that used to talk if you pulled her string, only she got broken a long time ago and if you try to dress her, her arm comes off. But I still like her. In fact, I still like most of them.

It's not that I want to play with them *all* the time or pretend I'm playing house or that I'm a *mother* or anything. But I just like kind of horsing around with them sometimes, talking to them. I took my microphone out.

"All right, Miss Gabbigale Ames," I said in my announcer voice. "How do you feel about being put in a big box in the back of the closet?"

"I wouldn't like it," I said in a squeaky doll voice.

"I'll take you out some of the time, only not when Libby's here," I explained in my regular voice.

"I'm scared of the dark," she said, or rather I said, pretending I was her. I had to keep changing voices so it would sound real.

I don't really blame her. I wouldn't want to be locked up in some dark old box either. "You know what the trouble with you is," I said. "You always wear dresses."

It's true. I never heard of a tomboy doll. Most of them come with dresses on.

Maybe Libby will change. She used to be one way so maybe she'll change again, not back to the old way, but to some different thing where she won't care so much about all this stuff. If she doesn't, I don't know what I'll do. I guess I won't have a best friend anymore.

4

Mom and Dad are going out tonight for dinner. They've been married twelve years so it's their anniversary. One thing I find hard to imagine is that Mom and Dad were married before I was born. I can imagine that they were once kids, but when I think of them together, I just imagine them as parents. I mean, I can't imagine them having just their regular names and no one calling them "Mom" or "Dad," because in a way those seem like their real names. I never really think of Mom as being "Bea," even though that's what her friends call her, and I'd never think of Dad as being "Chris," because that reminds me of Chris at school.

"Mom, can I have a sleepover date?" I asked her the night before.

"You mean, you going to someone's house or someone coming here?"

"Someone coming here."

"Sure, I don't see why not. You still want a baby-sitter, don't you?"

Maybe when I'm twelve or so I might stop wanting a baby-sitter, but now I still do. I know there's not much they could do if a robber or someone came, but I just don't like being alone in the house, even if one of my friends is there.

Jimmy said he could come. When he showed up, with his sleeping bag over his shoulder, Mom looked surprised. "Hi, Jimmy," she said. She took me aside and said, "I thought Libby was coming."

"No, I told you. She doesn't even like me anymore," I whispered. I didn't want Jimmy to hear.

"I guess at your age I never had sleepover dates with boys," Mom said.

"How come?"

"I don't know. I guess I was just too scared of boys."

Mom is always saying that, that she was really scared of boys when she was little. I don't see what there is to be scared of! "We won't stay up too late," I said.

"Do you want Dad to get out the folding bed?"

"No, he can just sleep in his sleeping bag."

When Mom and Dad had gone and the baby-sitter, this girl named Eloise Zaiken who goes to our school but is in eighth grade, came, Jimmy and I went into the kitchen to make a snack. Since I got to be ten, Mom says I can use the blender if I'm careful. We put in all this stuff— ice cream, milk, a banana, butterscotch sauce— and it turned out really good. We asked Eloise if she wanted some, but she said no. She said did we mind if her boyfriend came over and watched TV with her. We said we didn't care.

When we went into my room, Jimmy said, "Ugh! Who'd want *her* as a girlfriend?"

I giggled. "Maybe it's more like a friend who's a boy."

"No," he said. "We have a baby-sitter who asks if she can bring her boyfriend and they always end up kissing and stuff on the couch."

"How do you know?"

"Peter and I sneaked in and watched."

"Did they catch you?"

"Uh-uh."

"Were they saying all those things like I love you and darling and stuff?"

"I couldn't hear them that well."

I began thinking of this one time when I was six and I went into Mom and Dad's bedroom very early one morning. It wasn't the middle of the night, but it was still kind of dark out, and Dad was turned over on his side and he wasn't even wearing any pajamas! I've seen Mom lots of times without clothes, but never Dad. Really, all I saw was his tushy because I guess they heard me and pulled the covers up.

"Did you ever see your parents without their clothes on?" I asked.

Jimmy thought a minute. "You mean, like, really naked?"

"Yes."

"I've seen Dad sometimes."

"How about your mother?"

"Well, when Peter was born, she used to feed him so I saw her, you know, like, breasts . . . but I never saw *all* of her."

"Grownups look funny naked."

"I know. I don't know how they can stand to look at each other."

"I guess they usually take their clothes off when it's dark so they don't really see."

"Yeah, I guess so. Peter saw this girl naked once."

"How did he?"

"He said he'd give her three comics if she took her clothes off so she did. He said it wasn't so special."

"I don't see why people make such a big fuss about stuff like that, like it was dirty or something. My mother says it's not."

"My mother says you have to be ready for it, whatever that means."

"They always say that about everything."

"I guess she means if you start kissing people when you're too young, it might not be good, maybe you'd really hate it and you'd never want to do it again."

"Did you ever kiss anybody?"

"You mean, like, a girl?"

"Uh-huh."

"No! Some girls will punch you, if you do. They'll give you a black eye."

Jimmy went into the bathroom to change into his pajamas. I heard him lock the door. Maybe he was scared I'd come in and see him without any clothes on. I wouldn't even want to so he doesn't have to worry.

It was kind of cold and windy out. I remembered how when Libby used to sleep over we sometimes pretended we were Indian princesses and we would make a tent and sleep out on the terrace. But I knew Mom and Dad wouldn't let Jimmy and me sleep out there when it's so cold.

"What's the latest you ever stayed up?" Jimmy asked me when we were in bed.

"You mean straight up without falling asleep at all?"

"Uh-huh."

"I guess around eleven."

"I once stayed up till midnight," he said. "I wish I could stay up all night sometime."

"I bet you couldn't. You'd fall asleep."

"Uh-uh. I'd make myself stay awake—I know how."

"How?"

"You just keep thinking of different things and you don't let yourself close both eyes at once. You always keep one open."

"What if it just closes by itself?"

"You don't let it."

We talked some more and then we fell asleep. Usually I sleep right through the night unless I have a bad dream or something, but this time I heard Mom and Dad coming home. I think it was because William started barking. I got up and went out to say hello to them.

"Toe! Aren't you two sleeping yet?" Mom looked amazed. "It's nearly one."

"Jimmy is." I gave a big yawn. "I heard you come in. I was having this really funny dream." I know the dream was something about dogs, but when I tried to remember exactly what it was, I couldn't.

Dad went downstairs to put Eloise in a cab. I guess her boyfriend must've gone home.

"I wonder if Brendan will make it through the night," Mom said. "Maybe I better wake him, just to be on the safe side." If you don't wake him, he gets up really early, like five, which was not even that far away.

I went in with Mom and she woke Brendan up and changed him. He can hold his own bottle now, but he still likes it if you hold him.

When Dad came up, he said, "Is that baby eating again?"

Brendan went "Whump," which sounded like he was saying: I can eat if I want. Mom let me carry him back into bed. I stayed there a minute and played with him through the slats of his crib. He likes to grab my fingers and pretend to bite them. His teeth aren't too sharp so it doesn't really hurt.

5

I was good in volleyball today. That's practically the only sport I'm not terrible at. Afterward Libby said maybe I could come to their club meeting. I know I should have said, "Yuck, who wants to join your dumb old club," but I said I'd go. Anyway, clubs are always the same, just sitting around talking and stuff. It's worse if you're not in it, but if you are, it's usually not so special.

"I think Jimmy Sherrill has a crush on you," Florence said to me once we were in Libby's room, sitting on the floor.

"Yeah," said Ginny. "He talks to you more than to anybody! More than to the other *boys* even!"

"Did he sleep over at your house?" Libby said.

"Uh-huh," I said.

They all began to laugh.

I turned red. "Why shouldn't he have?" I said.

"Oh boy, you must really like him," Florence said.

"I don't," I said. "I mean, I like him, but I don't . . . it's not a romantic thing or anything."

I thought they might keep on teasing me, but luckily Ginny began talking about her sister who's going with this boy who she might marry and how he slept over one weekend and she saw him in his pajamas.

"How'd he look?" Libby said.

"Fat," Ginny said. "I don't even know why she likes him."

"*My* sister's having a baby," Florence said.

"I thought she already had one," Libby said.

"Yeah, only she wants another one."

"I'm never going to have one," Ginny said.

"Me neither," said Florence.

"Me neither," said Libby.

"It isn't even having to do all that stuff to have them," Ginny said. "They're just dumb. Babies are dumb."

"I bet Antonia's going to have one," Ginny said.

"I am not," I said.

"You and Jimmy Sherrill will probably have ten babies!" Ginny said and giggled.

"Quit it," I said. It made me feel really bad that Libby didn't even take my side or anything. She just let them tease me, like she didn't even care. Then they began making this list of all the girls in our class, dividing everyone into GG's (Girly Girls) and TB's (Tom Boys). It seems like, according to them, to be a real tomboy you have to promise you'll never get married and never have babies. I said I wouldn't, but really I'm not sure. How can you tell what you might want to do when you're older? You might change your mind.

I got home a little late, but I walked Hortense anyway. Mrs. Shorr asked if I had time to come in and have some milk and cookies. I guess I should've said no since it was close to dinner and it might've spoiled my appetite, but I said yes.

I told Mrs. Shorr about the Tomboy Club. She laughed. "Oh goodness," she said. "If you'd only seen me at your age! You'd have had to look pretty far to find more of a tomboy than I was."

"Really?" I said. It was sort of hard to imagine Mrs. Shorr as a tomboy.

"Of course, things were different then. . . . I loved dogs, just like you, and my mother thought that made me a tomboy. According to her, girls should like cats, and, oh, you know, perfectly harmless things, climbing trees, getting holes in your stockings, all of that."

"But did you all of a sudden get different?" I said.

"No. Well, I still like all those things," she said. "I haven't climbed too many trees lately, it's true. But I'm still fond of dogs, even of this old monster here."

Hortense was lying on the rug and she kind of rolled her eyes back, as though she heard what Mrs. Shorr said. I got down and began petting her. She has all these thick folds of skin around her neck that just kind of hang there. It's like she was supposed to be bigger, but never grew into all that skin.

"Did you have a lot of friends?" I said.

"When I was young?" Mrs. Shorr looked down at Hortense. "Oh, I had friends, animal friends, imaginary friends, but truth to tell, I didn't have a whole lot of friends my own age, if that's what you mean. My sisters were all much older than me, ten, fifteen years older. They thought of me as just a baby."

When I went to walk Freddie, I began wondering if maybe Libby would never really like me again. In the beginning I thought it was just happening for a little while, but that she'd change back. Now I don't think she'll ever change back.

6

"Toe, do me a favor and go down and get some more milk," Dad said. "I forgot to get some when I was out shopping before."

I went down to the supermarket near our house which is called Food Empire. It's big and everything is laid out so you can see it right away. I took the milk on the line for people who had less than ten things. While I was standing there, I looked down and saw this red line on my tights. I had rolled up my pants a little because they'd gotten wet from the snow and right near my foot was a red spot, like blood.

I got really scared. I'm sort of a coward about blood and stuff like that. I went upstairs, put the milk away, and went in the bathroom. My underpants were all kind of wet and had a big red spot on them. My heart was beating so fast I could hardly think. "Dad!" I called.

He didn't hear me. I went running into the bedroom. Dad was lying down and Brendan was in his playpen on the floor. "Did you get the milk?" Dad asked.

"Dad, I'm bleeding," I said. I started to cry.

"Where, honey?" Daddy sat up right away. "Show me."

I was too embarrassed to show him so I just explained.

"Well, don't you think . . . that sounds like it must be your period," Dad said. "Don't you think it sounds like that to you?"

"But I'm too young," I said. "I'm only ten."

"Ten does seem a little young," Dad said. "Maybe we should call Mom."

"Will she mind if you call her at work?"

"No, don't be silly." He went inside and I followed him. It's not that I don't know about girls getting their period, but I thought it was supposed to happen when you were much older, like twelve or thirteen.

It took a long time to get Mom on the phone and when she heard about it, she said, "Congratulations, sweetie! That's terrific. You know where the sanitary napkins are, don't you, honey?"

"But Mom, it's so soon!" I said. "I'm only ten."

"Well, ten's a *little* young, but I got mine then too. It must be some hereditary thing, getting it early. Don't worry, sweetie. Really."

I was really relieved to hear Mom say she got hers at ten too. But after we'd hung up, I still felt terrible. I didn't feel like I could explain it to Dad, how sometimes you're not ready for something to happen.

"Do you know how to . . . work everything?" Dad said, a little nervously. "Mom said she'd try and get home early."

I know where Mom keeps the sanitary napkins. They're in the linen closet with all the towels and my bike and roller skates and extra soap.

After I got it on, I went inside and lay down on the bed next to Dad. He smiled at me. "So, this is a pretty important day," he said.

I know he was trying to be nice, but all of a sudden I started to cry. I kept thinking how if Libby knew, she and Ginny and Florence would really make fun of me.

"Darling, what's wrong?" Daddy said, patting me. "Is it that you're nervous? Or scared?"

I wished I could explain what I felt to him. "I don't want to have a baby!" I said finally.

"Well, sweetheart, you're not going to have a baby."

"No, but I could."

"Sure, but—"

"Why does it happen so soon?" I never understood that, why it doesn't happen when you're sixteen or even twenty. "Nobody even *wants* to have a baby when they're eleven or ten so what's the point of it?"

Dad said that in some countries long ago people died much younger, like at thirty, so they started doing everything earlier, and having babies at thirteen or fourteen wasn't that unusual.

"But you know you don't just *have* a baby, don't you, Toe?" he said.

I nodded. It was just the idea! The idea that I *could* that was so awful! How could you be a tomboy at all if you could have a baby?

It was even worse when Mom came home. She'd stopped off to get this special cake and she began acting like it was this terrific thing. I was scared to tell her how I felt like it wasn't terrific at all. When I'd tried to tell her about the Tomboy Club, she'd thought it was just dumb. I was afraid she'd think the way I felt now was dumb, too.

"I know how you feel, Toe," she said. "But really, honey, it'll probably be very irregular in the beginning. That's how it was with me."

"I wish I didn't have to *ever* get it!" I said.

"But then you couldn't ever have a baby," Mom said. "Think how sad you'd feel."

"I wouldn't! I'd feel glad. I don't *want* to have one!"

"Well, honey, of course you don't want to have one *now*. But later you'll feel differently."

"I won't! I'm *never* going to."

She smiled. "Are babies all that terrible?"

I didn't know how to explain it. It wasn't babies, it was the whole thing of having to get breasts and have them flop around and the whole thing of boyfriends.

The thing I was most afraid of was that Libby

would find out. What if when we had gym she saw the sanitary napkin under my underpants or I had a funny smell or something? Mom said I could try using a tampon if I wanted, that that wouldn't smell so much because it was inside. "Would you like me to show you how to put it in?" she said.

"Okay," I said. But it seemed like I couldn't find the right place. I kept poking around and it wouldn't go in at all. "There isn't room," I said.

"Yes, there is. There's lots of room, sweetie."

"Not in *me*. . . . There just isn't."

"You're too nervous. Hon, look, it's the first time. I'm sure there won't be much blood. So let's forget about the tampon for a while. . . . Why don't we just sit down and have a nice dinner?"

We did sit down and have dinner, but even though Mom and Dad kept smiling and trying to be nice, I still felt awful. I couldn't even finish the chocolate cream cake Mom got to celebrate.

7

Jimmy is having a birthday party. He's going to be eleven. He invited me. He didn't send invitations—he called me up and asked if I wanted to come. He said his parents were taking him and some other kids from our class to this magic show and that we'd have dinner before at this special place called the Spaghetti House.

Mom came into my room when I was getting ready. "Hon, why don't you wear that nice patchwork skirt that Aunt Marjorie got you?"

"Oh, I don't want to that much," I said. "I'll just wear regular clothes."

"But it's a party!" Mom said.

"Mom, nobody gets all dressed up for parties! They just don't."

Mom sat down and watched as I pulled on my sweater. "When I was little we had to wear velvet dresses and tight patent leather shoes."

"Was that so great?" I said.

"No." She sighed. "But it seems like now it's going so much in the other direction."

"*You* never wear dresses," I pointed out.

"Yes, I do, sometimes. At night I wear long

skirts. I think when you're older you'll see it's fun to do all that, not to feel you *have* to maybe, but to get dressed up and look pretty."

"And wear perfume? Ugh." I think most perfumes stink.

"Is Libby going to the party?" Mom asked.

"I don't know," I said. "I don't know who he invited." I didn't think he'd invite Libby though— he said he doesn't like her that much.

"I was just thinking that if she did, maybe you could bring her home afterward and she could sleep over."

"Mom, I told you about a million times—Libby doesn't even like me anymore!"

"But I thought you said she let you come to that club she started."

I thought of how they were all teasing me and making fun of me. "I don't know if I'll go again," I said.

"Why not?"

"Oh, they think I like Jimmy just because he visits me sometimes or sleeps over."

Mom smiled. "He's a nice boy, Toe."

"I know! I like him, but it's not like he's my boyfriend!"

"Sure, no, I see what you mean."

"I just think he's a nice person. I don't see how that's so terrible."

"Well, it wouldn't be terrible if you liked him as a boyfriend either—eventually," Mom said.

"Yes, it would!"

"Why?"

"Because I hate all that!"

"All what?"

"Kissing and—you know."

"You'll like it in time," Mom said. "I'm not talking about now."

"I won't! I'm not going to *ever* like it."

I went over to her. "Mom, promise if you ever talk to Libby's mommy on the phone, you won't ever mention to her that I got my period."

"Sure," Mom said.

"Or to anyone, *ever*. Even to Aunt Marjorie."

"I don't get it," Mom said. "When I was your age, all the girls were looking forward to getting their period and being old enough to wear lipstick and stockings and go to dances. You wouldn't want to be ten years old forever, would you?"

"Yes, I would," I said. I meant it, too.

"Honey, what a thought! There are such good things ahead."

"How do you know?"

"I know." But actually being nine was better in some ways. When I was nine, Libby still liked me, even if I wasn't good at sports, and I was still an only child and I didn't have my period.

I took the bus to Jimmy's house. I was a little late so everybody was already waiting in the lobby. Jimmy's mother said I should give her the present and Jimmy would open them at the restaurant. I got him the Photos from Star Trek because he said that's what he wanted. I think when you're little, you more want to be surprised, but when you're older you want to get some particular thing.

There were only five of us—me, Jimmy, these two boys from our class, Henry Larrabee and Abie Fine, and some other boy named Larry whom Jimmy had met in camp. I didn't mind that much being the only girl because no one seemed to care or notice or make a big fuss. The only thing I didn't like that much was the spaghetti. It was that gloppy white kind with red tomato sauce over it that looked sort of like blood. I like the kind that's more hard and you just put butter and cheese on. I sort of mushed it around my plate so no one would notice I didn't eat that much. The cake was terrific. It had this Star Trek design which Jimmy's mother told the store to put on, with real spaceships and everything. You didn't really want to cut into it and spoil it.

When we went to the magic show, we got into two different cabs. I was in the one with Larry and Abie and Jimmy's father. Jimmy's father sat in the front seat next to the cab driver.

"Can you do magic tricks?" Larry asked.

"I can do some," I said. When Mattie was three,

I did some tricks for her friends, but of course they're little so they didn't notice if something went wrong.

Abie said, "My kid brother wrecked this magic set I got. He got it all mixed up and now it doesn't work anymore."

"I put mine way up high in the closet," I said, "so my brother can't get it."

"They always end up getting it," Abie said. "They climb up on ladders or something."

"I don't have a brother," Larry said. "Or a sister either."

"Lucky!" Abie said.

"Yeah, I like it. Everybody else feels sorry for me."

"I used to be an only child," I said, "till I was ten. But Brendan isn't so bad."

"That's just because he's still little," Abie said. "Then they don't have teeth and they can't walk. It's when they start climbing all over stuff and breaking things that it gets really bad."

"How come Jimmy invited you?" Larry said.

"Why shouldn't he have?" I said.

"Because you're a girl."

"He likes her," Abie said and guffawed.

"So! He likes you too," I said.

"Are you his girlfriend?" Larry said.

"No! I'm not his or anyone's."

"I have two girlfriends," Larry said. "One's in my class and one lives in my building."

"Two girlfriends!" Abie made a face. "Yuck!"

"Yeah, we go square dancing and stuff."

"I hate girls," Abie said.

"Thanks a lot," I said.

"Not you especially. But, well, they're always whispering and making fun of people," Abie said. "Like your friend, Libby."

It's true, Libby does make fun of people, but that's just the way she is, it's not because she's a girl. "She does that to everybody," I said.

"I bet she doesn't do it to other girls."

"Yes, she does," I said. "I know! She even does it to me!"

"Yeah, we have a girl like that in our class," Larry said. He was one of these very calm people who you could tell wouldn't mind if someone teased him. He just wouldn't pay attention probably. I wish I was like that.

The magic show was really good. Nobody, not even Jimmy's parents, could figure out how they did all those things. It didn't look like there was a trapdoor or any special box for people to hide in. Maybe it was real magic, not just tricks. Jimmy said no, that it was tricks, but even professional magicians couldn't figure it out.

When I got home, Mom and Dad were in pajamas, watching TV. It was late, around eleven, only I didn't feel at all sleepy.

"How was it?" Dad asked.

"Great."

"Did Libby come?"

"Uh-uh. I was the only girl. I didn't mind, though." I jumped on the bed next to them. "What're you watching?"

It was just the news, which looked sort of dull, so I said good night to them and went in to bed.

8

I think my father is pretty good about most things. He can be strict, but he usually tries to explain to you what he's being strict about. He doesn't just start screaming and yelling for no reason. But about this one thing we had kind of a fight. It was about this. Ms. Portion, our teacher, said that next week she thought it would be interesting if some of the fathers of the kids in our class, the ones that could get away, would come in and describe their professions to us, what they did at work, because we're studying the working world.

"That sounds like an interesting idea," Dad said when I told him and Mom about it at dinner. "Okay, sign me up for Tuesday."

"But Dad, you don't *have* a job."

"I used to, doesn't that count? Can't I talk about what I used to do?"

"Uh-uh."

"Okay, I'll talk about what I do now."

"But you don't *do* anything now. You're just, you know, unemployed."

"Toe, how can you say that?" Mom said. "Dad

does millions of things. He looks after Brendan, he takes care of the laundry. . . ."

"But those aren't real things! That's not real *work*."

"What is it, then?"

"It's not *real*! Work is when you go somewhere and get paid. Looking after babies isn't the same."

"Listen," Dad said. "I'm the expert. I've done both and I can tell you, looking after Brendan is work. Believe me. I'll bring him in and they'll see."

"That'll wreck everything," I said. I knew Brendan would crawl around chewing on things and maybe ripping up people's homework. It would be terrible.

"What I want to know," Mom said, "is why this project is just confined to fathers? Why can't mothers come in and talk about *their* work?"

"Mom, you *know* why. Because they don't work—most of them."

"Libby's mother does, Abie Fine's mother is a—"

"But that's just a couple. It wouldn't be enough for a real project."

"Let them come in the same week as the fathers. One day some fathers and some mothers, mixed in."

"That's not the way Ms. Portion wants to do it. . . . She only wants fathers. Mom, maybe in the spring they'll have it for mothers."

"The more I hear of this, the less I like," Mom said.

Dad said, "Not me, *I'm* not scared. Brendan and I are coming in Tuesday."

"Well, then I won't go to school," I said.

"Honey!"

"They'll make fun of me! Get a baby-sitter for him, Dad? Please."

"Nope. We're a package. They take us together or not at all."

"I don't think babies are even allowed in school," I said.

"How come?"

"They might, you know, get germs and stuff."

"We'll chance it."

I kept hoping that maybe I would get a terrible cold so I couldn't go to school that day, but I didn't. Dad said he was going to bicycle across the park with Brendan in the backseat and he'd see me at ten. On Monday there had been three fathers—Abie's who's a dentist and Caleb's who's a policeman and Michael's who's a doctor, but the kind for grownups, not for children. They were all pretty good except for the dentist, who kept telling us about how to brush our teeth and even handed out toothbrushes! Like we were babies! If I was Abie, I would've been ashamed, but he didn't seem to mind that much.

Dad asked Ms. Portion if it was all right if

Brendan crawled around on the floor while he talked. She said sure.

"He crawls backward," I said. "He hasn't learned the regular way yet."

"Well, I think I have quite an unusual profession," Dad said, sitting on this chair next to Ms. Portion.

"You're an engineer, I believe?" Ms. Portion said. She must have known that because of these cards they make you fill out at the beginning of each year where they say where your parents work and their phone number in case you get sick.

"I *used* to be an engineer," Dad said, "but this year I'm taking off to be at home." He began telling about the stuff he and Brendan do during the day. Some of the kids asked questions.

"What if you have to change his diaper?" Louisa Munth said.

"I change it," Dad said, smiling. "Diapers aren't too complicated."

"But my father says they stink," she said. "He says women don't mind it, but men do."

"My daddy changes diapers," Caleb said.

"So does mine," said someone else.

"Yeah, but where do you learn all that stuff?" Michael asked.

"You pick it up," Dad said. "It's not all that complicated."

"I bet you wish you didn't have to," Louisa said.

"I don't know if I'd want to do this all my life," Dad said, "but it's been an interesting change. I'm glad I had the chance to do it."

"I imagine it must be interesting for Antonia," Ms. Portion said.

I was sort of scrunched down in the back of the room, hoping no one would see me. I kept looking at Brendan, who was circling around. He'd picked up some wooden piece from one of our math sets and was licking it.

"Toe is a big help to me," Dad said. "Without her it would be much harder."

That made me feel sort of ashamed, because lots of times when Dad has asked me to help with Brendan, I've said I wouldn't or I was too busy.

"I wonder how many other children in the class help their mothers and fathers with their baby brothers and sisters," Ms. Portion said. "I'm sure Antonia can't be the only one."

"Me and my father cook Sunday dinner," Abie said. "But my brother can't come in because he might fiddle with the stove or play with matches."

"I do the bathroom," said Florence, "on Saturday morning. Only we don't have any babies in our family."

Everyone began talking about stuff they did

at home with their baby brothers or sisters. Brendan crawled over to where I was sitting. He pulled himself up on his knees. "To-to-uh," he said, which means he wanted me to hold him in my lap. "To-to" is what he calls me and "uh" means up. You wouldn't think "p" would be too hard to say, but I guess it is for him. I let him sit in my lap and hoped he wouldn't make too much noise. But just then, when it was quiet for a minute, he put his finger on my nose and said loudly, "No." Everyone turned around to look at us.

"That means nose," I said. "He's just learning to talk."

Brendan put his finger in my mouth. I kept my lips closed because if I don't, he puts his whole hand in practically. He likes to feel my teeth. "Muh," he said.

"That must mean mouth," Ms. Portion said.

Then he poked at one of my eyes and said with this big grin, "Eye!"

"Well, what a smart baby," said Ms. Portion. "I can see he's going to be as smart as his sister someday."

Ms. Portion isn't married and doesn't have a baby so she doesn't know that all babies can say things like that, even dumb ones.

When Dad left with Brendan I looked out the window and watched them bicycling away.

Gretchen came over and stood next to me. "Your father is nice," she said.

"He is pretty nice most of the time," I said. I didn't want it to sound like I was boasting or anything!

That night Dad said, "So, did we disgrace you terribly, Toe?"

I shrugged my shoulders. "It was okay."

"Personally, I think Brendan was the hit of the show," Dad said.

"Yeah, he was pretty good."

9

Today is Elvira's birthday. She's fourteen years old. That makes her almost like a great-grandmother. I was in this sort of silly mood so I brought my microphone in to interview her. "Today we have with us on Channel WTAT Ms. Elvira Henderson, one of the oldest dogs on West 86th Street. How do you feel today, Elvira?"

Elvira was just lying there the way she usually does. She's not that playful anymore. If I try to interview William, he goes jumping around, barking. "You're feeling pretty good? Well, our audience is glad to hear that. You're looking good, too. All right, let's have a big hand for our guest of the day, the cutest Yorkshire terrier for miles around, Ms. Elvira Henderson!"

Mom came through the dining room and said, "Toe, leave her alone, will you?"

"I'm just interviewing her, for her birthday."

"I thought you said you were going to take those dolls over to Libby's house this afternoon."

"I am. I'm still trying to decide which ones to give away."

Actually, that wasn't true. I'd decided a long time ago that the ones I really don't like so much anymore are the little Raggedy Ann and Hetty who has this watch that used to tell time and some old Barbies that look kind of grungy because they're so old.

Mom was in the kitchen getting out some cereal. "Can I make my own egg?" I said.

"Okay," Mom said.

Eggs are my specialty. I make them three ways—sunny-side up, sunny-side down, and sunny-side all over. Sunny-side all over means you break the yolk on purpose after the egg is in the pan by poking at it with a fork. I like those best.

"Elvira *is* pretty old," I said.

"I know," Mom said. "I remember when I met Dad. I'd just had her for a year or so and she was so jealous of him! Whenever he sat down next to me on the couch, she'd start to growl."

"Mom?"

"What?"

"Did you know the minute you met Dad that you wanted to marry him?"

"No!" Mom smiled. "How could I?"

"But on TV they always do. They just look at someone and they can tell."

"Oh, you can tell you think someone looks nice, but I think you can't really fall in love till you get to know them. And sometimes you can be in love with someone, but not want to marry them."

"You can?"

"Sure. I was in love with a couple of people before I met Dad."

I never knew that! What if Mom had married one of those people? I wouldn't even ever have been born!

"Sometimes I feel like Elvira was my first child," Mom said, smiling. "She was such a tiny fluff of a thing when I got her. So cuddly and cute, like a kitten."

"She's not that cute anymore," I said.

"I know. But I still love her."

I don't think I do love Elvira, not the way Mom does. Maybe that's because I only knew her when she was old. Most of the time she just sleeps near the radiator. If William wants to fool around with her, she barks at him, even though he's so much bigger than her. I think he's scared of her.

I went over to Libby's house without even calling. I should have called, but I was scared Libby would say I shouldn't come. Libby's mother came to the door. She was still in her bathrobe, even though it was almost twelve.

"Oh, hi, Antonia," she said. "Goodness, I haven't seen you in such a long time."

I guess she forgot that time I was over for the

club. Maybe she meant I hadn't come over just by myself the way I used to. "I brought these dolls for Mattie," I said. "I don't use them so much anymore."

"Five of them? She'll be out of her head! Do you really want to give them all away? Some of them look almost new."

"Well, I don't play with dolls anymore," I said loudly, just in case Libby was listening.

"Isn't that funny? Libby doesn't either. I guess it puzzles me because I just loved dolls when I was the age of you two."

"Is, um, Libby home?" I asked.

"She's inside watching TV. Let me go get her. Mattie! Libby!"

Mattie came running out in around one second. "Look, Bunches, see what Antonia brought for you—some new dolls."

Mattie looked at me. "Why?" she said.

"They're kind of . . . I don't play with them so much anymore," I said. "I guess I'm more interested in sports and stuff like that."

Mattie took the dolls and looked at me like she couldn't believe it. "Can I keep them forever?" she said.

"Sure. I might bring some more over some other time," I said.

"Libby!" Mattie shrieked. "Look what Toe brought me! Look!"

Libby came out of the bedroom. She was still in her pajamas too. "Ugh—dolls," she said when she saw what Mattie was carrying.

"Well, I think that's terribly thoughtful of you, Antonia," Libby's mother said. "Mattie really appreciates it. Don't you, sweetheart?"

Mattie was too busy playing with the dolls to even hear her.

"I'm watching a baseball game," Libby said. "Want to watch?"

"Okay."

I went inside and we sat on the floor watching the game. I remember how when we were little we used to watch *The Electric Company* and *Sesame Street*. Libby seemed to know all about the baseball game, who to root for and which players were good. I just sat there, not knowing too much what was going on, but sort of pretending I did.

10

Something horrible happened last week. I wasn't at home when it happened, which is good because I wouldn't have wanted to see it. It seems like Elvira knocked into this iron gate we have between the living room and the hall. There was a prong sticking out and it went right through her eye! Dad took her right away to the Animal Medical Center and they bandaged it up. But now she just barks all the time, all day, in this sort of whining way.

"It can't be healing properly," Mom said when we were having breakfast one day.

"We have to give it a week at least," Dad said. "It may take a little longer for the healing process since she's so old."

"I wish she'd stop barking," I said.

"She's in pain!" Mom yelled. "She's barking because she's in pain!" She marched into the kitchen and slammed the door.

I looked down at my plate. I hadn't meant anything bad.

"Toe, listen," Dad said in a quiet voice. "Mom

is very upset because, you know, she loves Elvira a lot."

"I know," I said. I looked up at him. "Do you love her a lot?"

"No, not really," he said. "I'm fond of her, but I don't love her."

"How come?"

"Well, I don't feel the same way about animals that Mom does. She always loved them and I, well, I don't *not* like them, but I don't have that kind of special feeling."

"She said Elvira was like her first child," I said.

"Exactly. She was living alone for the first time and so, for some people a dog can be a lot of things, a friend or a child, someone to take care of."

I remember how sometimes when Mom is in the kitchen by herself, I'll hear her talking to Elvira. If you catch her at it, she always gets embarrassed. "Will she stop barking?" I said.

"I hope so," said Dad. "But, till she does, let's try to kind of ignore it as best we can."

"But I can't!" I said. "I hear her all the time!"

"Just close the door."

"I do. I can still hear her."

"What do you mind about it—the noise or that she's in pain?"

"I guess both." It was like hearing someone crying all the time. You'd think you would get used to it, but you don't.

"Remember when you were four and Grandma was staying with us? Remember how she had those hiccups all the time because she was so sick and you used to come into our room at night?"

I didn't remember. I remember coming into Mom and Dad's room, but I can't remember Grandma that well. "Can I sleep in your room till she stops?" I said.

Dad sighed. "Sweetie, you're ten. You're too old for that."

"But I get scared when I hear her. Please, Dad? I can just sleep on the floor in my sleeping bag."

"Well, let me talk about it with Mom."

Mom said it was ridiculous and that I should just try and not notice.

I tried, but at night I still hear Elvira barking and it seems like it sounds even louder than it does during the day.

11

I still get worried that sometime Libby will find out I got my period. In gym when we have to change I try to go into the bathroom. Lots of times there are jokes about people smelling bad and I never even cared about them before, but now I keep thinking that I might really smell. It's like Elvira barking—it seems like I notice it so much that I can't tell if it really is so bad or it's just my imagination.

I went ice skating with Jimmy after school when I got my period the third time. I kept thinking that maybe the blood would leak through or something, even through my tights, and I kept going into the bathroom to check. I don't know which would be more embarrassing, having Jimmy find out or having Libby find out. Boys are lucky. I mean, they don't have to worry about stuff like getting their period. It seems like it's easier for them. I don't know if I'd want to *be* a boy, but I wish I didn't have to get my period till I really wanted to have a baby. I wish it was something that only happened after you'd decided you wanted a baby, but if you didn't want one, you didn't have to get it. In school they said it was like a nest was being built inside you and then falling apart if it wasn't needed. But I don't see any point to keep on having nests built if you're not going to use them! Dad says nature is so efficient, but it seems to me that she could have done it some other way. Well, at least I'm glad I don't live in one of those places where girls have babies when they're fourteen and die when they're thirty or so. I don't think I would even like to visit a place like that!

In biology our teacher said the body goes through changes when it's ready. She said, "There's a time for everything," and if something happens, it's because the time has come for it to happen. I started thinking about that. I don't know if I agree. It seems to me some things just happen, not especially at the right time. I think they just say that the way Dad says nature is so efficient, but really it doesn't make that much sense.

At the next meeting of the Tomboy Club, Florence said, "I think Mrs. Tyroler is dumb! I hate the way she keeps saying it's so wonderful to get your period and all that stuff about nests."

"Well, you do have to get it," Ginny said. "You just do."

"When my sister used to get hers," Florence said, "she'd be sick for a whole week."

Everyone looked nervous.

"Was there a lot of blood?" Libby asked. She's even more scared of blood than me.

"Yes! She had to even stay in bed all day there was so much. And she had terrible stomachaches, too."

"But Mrs. Tyroler said most people don't have them."

"Well, Alice did. She *still* gets them, and she's married!"

"I wonder why she gets them."

Libby's mother came in the room. "Girls, I've got your hot chocolate all ready," she said. "Come on in."

"Oh, can't we have it in here, Mom?" Libby said. "Please!"

"It'll just get all over the rug, Libby. I have it all set out. Three with whipped cream, one without."

"Is it real whipped cream?" Florence said.

"No," Libby said. "It comes from a can."

Before Mom started working, she used to whip the real kind of cream. I like that better than the other kind which you squirt out of a can. That kind reminds me of shaving cream.

We all sat in the kitchen at this long table, on stools, having hot chocolate and Oreos. Mattie wasn't there. She was visiting someone evidently.

"Girls, don't get all upset about getting your period," Libby's mother said. "It's hardly ever painful. That's very rare. And the blood is minor. You get used to it."

"Mom!" Libby said. "Were you eavesdropping on us?" She looked really mad.

"Never," Libby's mother said, smiling. "Cross my heart and hope to die. I was just innocently walking in to call you for hot chocolate."

"We're not scared of the *blood*," Ginny said. "But we just wish we didn't have to go through all that stuff. Boys don't."

"Well, boys go through changes at that age, too," Libby's mother said. "It's just a part of growing up."

"It's easier for them," Libby said. "I wish *I* was a boy."

"Me too," Ginny said.

"I wish I was a horse," Florence said.

"I wish I was a dog," I said.

"Hmm," Libby's mother said. "These choices are getting interesting. I wonder what I should pick."

"You wish you were a mother, probably," Libby said, sighing.

"Yes, I guess I do."

"Mothers and fathers always just want to be what they are," Libby said.

"*I* used to wish I was a boy," Libby's mother said.

"Then how come you stopped?" Ginny said.

"Well, I suppose . . . I don't know. That's a good question, Ginny. I don't know exactly *when* I stopped wishing it. I guess once I began to feel there wasn't anything I could do as a boy that I couldn't do as a girl."

"But that's not true!" Libby said. "Boys can do more things!"

"Phooey!" Libby's mother said. "That's just an excuse."

We all went back to Libby's room after our snack, but luckily they didn't talk anymore about people getting their period. I was really glad because I kept thinking someone would ask, "Did you ever get yours?" and we would have to go around and swear to tell the truth or drop dead that second.

I was the last person to go home. Mom had said she would stop by for me on her way home from work because she wanted to talk to Libby's mother. Being there alone with Libby was much nicer than being there with the whole club. It's not just that I don't like Ginny and Florence, but I like being with just one person better.

"Do you still have Regina?" I asked. Regina was this huge paper doll Libby had that had lots of clothes, some with real lace and buttons on them. We used to sit around trimming things out for her. Like we'd trim out some meat and mushroom casserole and paste it on cardboard for her food. And we'd make a pocketbook and trim out real lipsticks and perfume and face cream and put them in it.

"Her head's sort of wobbly," Libby said. "I let Mattie use her sometimes."

I told Libby about Elvira and her barking.

"Boy, that would drive me crazy!" Libby said. "Sometimes Mattie gets sick and keeps blowing her nose all night. I can't get to sleep."

"Brendan can't even *blow* his nose," I said. "He doesn't know how! You have to blow it for him."

"Is she going to bark that way all the time?" Libby asked. Libby likes dogs, just like me, even though they don't have one.

"I guess it's because her eye hurts her," I said.

"I hate to think about that," Libby said, making a face.

"Me too."

"I hate it when people are, you know, like really sick."

"I know. William keeps looking at her, like he can tell something's wrong, but he doesn't know what to do."

"Dogs can tell things like that," Libby said. "They really can."

"I know they can," I said. "They're smarter than people about some things."

"Well," Libby said, "I hope she gets better, Toe."

That was one of the first nice things Libby had said to me in months. "I do too."

"Maybe I'll make her a get-well card," Libby said. And she started drawing this really pretty card for Elvira. Mattie came in. She still had her sweater on.

"What's that?" she said, looking at what Libby was drawing.

"It's a dog," Libby said, still drawing. "It's a get-well card for Toe's dog."

"Is she sick?" Mattie said.

"Uh-huh," I said.

"Dogs can't be sick!" Mattie said and laughed.

"Yes, they can, stupid! Just like people," Libby said.

"Mommy said you shouldn't call me stupid," Mattie said.

"So! Don't say dumb things."

"I want to make her a get-well card too," Mattie said.

"You don't even know her," Libby said.

"I do so! She came to our house once," Mattie said.

That was true. When Mom used to pick me up earlier, before she began working, sometimes she'd bring William and Elvira.

"Your dogs don't even look like dogs," Libby said. "They look like hippos."

"They do not!" Mattie said.

"Have it your way," said Libby.

Actually, Mattie's dog did look a little like a hippo, but I thought it was nice of her to make one. When we got home, I showed Elvira the two cards, but she just kept barking. So I just put them there, next to the place where she sleeps. I don't know if she really understood they were especially for her.

12

Saturday morning I got up early to walk Freddie and Hortense. I walked Freddie first because the Bergsons like me to come exactly at nine. Mrs. Shorr doesn't care so much as long as it's before eleven. That's because she has the doorman walk Hortense late at night.

"How's Elvira doing?" Mrs. Shorr asked. I'd told her about Elvira's eye.

"She's sort of the same," I said.

"I'm sorry to hear that," Mrs. Shorr said.

"She's quite old," I said. Then I wondered if that might not have been so polite because Mrs. Shorr is rather old herself.

"Yes, things heal more slowly when you get older," Mrs. Shorr said. She still had her bathrobe on. It's sort of fancy. Her daughter got it for her and she says it's not so much her taste, but it wouldn't be polite to take it back to the store.

"I don't know if she barks about her eye because she's old," I said. "If it happened to William, he probably wouldn't like it either." I told her about how Libby and Mattie made get-well cards for Elvira.

"Libby's your best friend, is she?" Mrs. Shorr said.

"Well, sort of," I said. "She used to be."

"Oh? What happened?"

I didn't know if Mrs. Shorr would understand. "See, Libby thinks I don't act tomboyish enough," I said.

"Tomboyish *enough*!" said Mrs. Shorr. "When I acted like a tomboy, everybody chewed me out about it for weeks!"

Grownups use expressions like "chewed me out." I used to write them all down in this special book. "She wants to, you know, be a boy and stuff like that."

Mrs. Shorr sighed. "Oh yes! I remember all that. You want to know something, Antonia? When I was, well, a little younger than you, I was told or maybe I somehow got it in my head that if I went to sleep lying on my side, I'd wake up a boy."

I laughed.

"Crazy, isn't it? But I did it, night after night, always expecting that miraculous change to have taken place by the morning."

"I don't think Libby would do that!" I said. "She knows better."

"I would hope so! But it's always sad, isn't it,

when a friend gets that way? There's not much you can do about it, is there?"

I shook my head.

"You always think, 'What did I do wrong?' and it's never that you *did* anything wrong! People just change and you accept it, that's all."

"I have some other friends," I said, "like Jimmy, but he's not so much my *best* friend."

"One needs a best friend," Mrs. Shorr said. "No doubt about it."

"Do you think a boy can be a best friend?"

"Hmm? Well, maybe. . . . Maybe nowadays. But it's harder, isn't it? People always go at you about it. Dear, shouldn't you be going back home? I'm afraid your parents might worry if you stay out so long."

Actually, I hadn't realized it was so late. "They don't worry about me so much," I said. "They know I'll come back."

But when I got back home, only Dad was there. That was odd because on weekends Mom always takes me to a movie or something special since I don't see her so much during the week.

"Hi, Dad," I said. "Is Mom lying down?"

"No, she's out."

"Where'd she go?" I said. All of a sudden I realized it was really quiet in the apartment. I couldn't hear Elvira barking.

"She went out. Toe, come here one second."

"What?"

"Well, it's about Elvira."

"She's not barking anymore," I said.

"She's not here."

"Did Mom take her someplace?"

"Yes, you see . . . Well, we've talked it over with the doctors and they seem to think it best if she's put to sleep."

"What do you mean?"

"Didn't you ever hear that expression—to put a dog to sleep?"

"Uh-uh."

"Well, what it means is, if an animal, a dog or a cat or whatever, is just too sick or too old and you know they can't possibly get any better, then you give them a shot and they go to sleep."

"When they wake up, are they better?"

"No, they don't wake up. It's, well, permanent."

"You mean, just like killing them?"

"It's not killing, darling. It's a solution that you take only when you know absolutely and for certain the animal can't get better, that all they'll suffer is pain and more pain, and if you love them, you don't want that."

"But do they *know*?"

"What do you mean, do they know?"

"Do they know what's going to happen?"

"Well, no. Not in the way a person can. That's

good, really. In that way perhaps animals live more happily than people, more simply anyway, because they don't know what death is."

"But she ought to know!" I cried.

"Why?"

"What if she wouldn't want it?"

"Darling, listen. An animal isn't a person. I'm not saying they're better, worse, smarter, dumber, but things mean different things to them. Now you know how much Mom loves Elvira, don't you?"

I bit my lip. I nodded.

"You know she wouldn't ever do anything to hurt her or that she felt Elvira wouldn't want?"

"Yeah, I guess so."

"Toe, what's wrong? Do you really think Mom would do something that wasn't good for Elvira?"

"But it's like killing her, Dad." I didn't want to cry because that would've been babyish.

"It isn't. I don't know, Toe. Please try to understand. Because if you find this hard to accept, think of what it's like for Mom."

"Is it like when our baby died?"

Before she had Brendan, Mom had this baby who only lived two days because he was too small. He was born before he was supposed to. "It's a little the same. Of course, you feel differently, more intensely about a baby, you can understand that, can't you?"

I nodded.

"But, on the other hand, Mom didn't really know our baby. She's lived with Elvira all these years. You can't compare the two things. They're both sad things that happened and have to be accepted."

"I wish I never had to die," I said. I sat next to him. "I don't want you or Mom to *ever* die."

"Mom and I will be around for a good long time. That's the point about Elvira, too. She had a long life, she had lots of good times, she did all the things dogs like to do."

"She never had babies," I pointed out. I remember how Mom used to say Elvira would get this thing called a false pregnancy, which meant milk would come out of her nipples and she'd think she was pregnant, but she really wouldn't be.

"No, that's true. But lots of people don't have babies either."

"Maybe she wished she had them."

"Maybe. But dogs aren't like people, hon. Try to understand that. They don't wish for things the way you do. And, as I say, maybe that makes life easier for them."

"Is it happening right now?" I asked, snuggling as close to Dad as I could.

"Yes."

We sat there together, quietly. Dad kept

stroking my hair. "Elvira will just fall asleep in Mom's arms," he said. "Perfectly peacefully."

I know what Dad said is right, but I hated to think about it. If I were Mom, I don't think I could do that, sit there with Elvira in my arms, knowing she wouldn't wake up, ever. When we were in the country once I got friendly with this girl named Anita Goldberg and she said she had a dog that got run over. That would be even worse. He wasn't even old especially either. He was just playing around in the yard and ran out to chase a ball. Well, at least we still have William. I guess he'll be around for a long time.

13

I wonder if William knows that Elvira is gone. Of course, he can't understand what happened to her, but sometimes he'll go over to this place where she used to sleep near the radiator and he'll sniff around there and then look up at me, as though wondering why she isn't there.

"Maybe he can smell her," I said to Mom. In the beginning I didn't talk about Elvira that much to Mom because Dad said she would be sensitive about it, but now that it happened two months ago, I do sometimes.

"I'm sure he does," Mom said. "Dogs are very aware of things like that."

It was hard to tell if William liked Elvira that much. When he was a puppy, he used to try and get her to play. He'd jump all around and paw at her and lick her, which is like kissing her, but she'd just look up at him like she wished he would quit bothering her. Sometimes she'd growl at him. He never seemed to mind. He'd stop doing it, but then sometime later he'd come over again, as though he hoped she might be in a better mood. Maybe he was jealous of her because Mom would let her get up on the bed and sleep there. William was so big, Mom and Dad never wanted him to get in the habit of leaping on the couch and stuff.

William plopped down on the floor and kept looking at us. I wished so much I knew what he was thinking. I wonder if dogs can remember things, like when William is sniffing whether a picture comes in his mind of Elvira the way I can picture Libby even when she's not there or if it's more just a feeling.

When I walk William, sometimes I meet people who live in our neighborhood. Some of them ask about Elvira. Usually I just say she died of old age, which is partly true because she was very old. There's this one dog named Sasha who's a Yorkshire terrier just the way Elvira was. She was the only other dog Elvira seemed to like. When she'd see her coming, she'd wag her tail and run over, which she never did with other dogs. And Sasha would wag her tail and they'd kind of sniff at each other. Now, if I see Sasha coming, I sometimes cross over to the other side of the street.

"Mom, I'm going to walk Hortense now," I said.

"Okay, hon." Mom was getting ready to give Brendan his lunch. "See you later."

But when I came to Mrs. Shorr's apartment and rang the bell, this other woman answered it.

I figured it was Mrs. Shorr's daughter because Mrs. Shorr has all these pictures on her bureau of her daughter and grandchildren. The woman looked sort of surprised to see me.

"Who are you?" she said in this sort of sharp voice, like I might be a robber. She ought to know someone my age wouldn't be a robber!

"I came to walk Hortense," I said.

"Oh my God, yes, you're the little girl—Frank, the little girl is here, the one who helped Mother with Hortense."

I saw Hortense's leash hanging on the closet door like it always was. It's very short and made of leather. Hortense has a chain collar so you can try and pull her away when she's trying to eat garbage. She can pull pretty hard, though. Once, she pulled me so hard I fell right down! "Is Mrs. Shorr here?" I said.

"No, she's in the hospital," the woman said. "It's her heart."

"Oh," I said.

"She had another attack."

One of my uncles once had a heart attack, but now he's all right. "Is she okay?" I asked.

"They're doing all they can," she said.

I guess by "they" she meant the doctors. "Do you want me to walk Hortense?" I said. I could see her lying on the rug in the next room. When she saw me, she got up and ambled over, like she wanted to go out.

"You might as well," the woman said. "I'm Mrs. Jacoby, by the way. I'm Muriel's daughter."

"I'm Antonia Henderson," I said. "I live in this building."

"I know. Well, it's been very nice of you, dear, to look after Hortense this way. We appreciate it very much."

"That's okay," I said. "I like dogs."

While I was walking Hortense, I started wondering if I could visit Mrs. Shorr in the hospital. Probably they wouldn't let me. When Mom had Brendan, they wouldn't let children up, even to see their own brothers or sisters. Dad said there are some hospitals that are different, but that usually you have to be at least twelve. I am fairly big for my age. I could say I was twelve. Anyway, I think I'll make her a get-well card when I get home. Mom got these new markers, which are really pretty colors, yellow, green, and purple.

When I came upstairs again, Mrs. Jacoby was crying and her husband said, "Take it easy, Sallie. Go in and take a Miltown."

"I brought Hortense back," I said.

"Mrs. Shorr didn't make it," he said.

"You mean she died?"

He nodded.

I couldn't understand it. My uncle had a heart attack and now he's fine and says he feels as good as new and even plays tennis. I swallowed. I felt really bad. I never even got to write Mrs. Shorr a get-well card or anything. I never even knew she was going to get sick! I guess she was quite old since she had eight grandchildren, but she never *looked* that old. She dyed her hair this brown color and she wore bright-colored dresses so you couldn't tell.

Hortense was sitting next to me, scratching herself. "What will happen to Hortense?" I asked.

"God, I don't know," he said, looking down at Hortense as though he'd forgotten all about her.

"We can't keep her," Mrs. Jacoby said. She'd gone inside but now she came back again. "You know we can't, Frank."

"Sallie, you've got to calm down," he said.

"It's my mother!" she said, starting to cry.

"I know it's your mother . . . I know that."

It's strange to see a grownup woman crying about her mother.

"You see, our daughter, Angela, is allergic to dog hair," Mr. Jacoby said. "We had her for several years before we realized that. We had Angela tested for all kinds of allergies and finally it came out that it was Hortense. That's why we gave her to— Now Angela's much better and we just can't—"

"Oh, we'll get rid of her!" Mrs. Jacoby said. "We'll find a way." She sounded angry, maybe because Hortense had made her daughter get all those allergies.

Suddenly I got this terrible idea. I wondered if maybe they would put Hortense to sleep! She's not even that old, just around ten. "I can take her," I said.

They both looked at me. "Could you?" Mr. Jacoby said. "Permanently? Well, that would be wonderful, that would be just ideal."

"She's really a very fine dog," Mrs. Jacoby said, sniffing. "Did Mother ever show you her pedigree? It's incredible! Show dogs on every side. Her mother was—do you remember the name of her mother, Frank? I just can't think of it right now, but her mother was really famous, she won all kinds of ribbons. Hortense would have been a show dog too, but she has that patch on her coat. It's hardly noticeable really, but they said it would, you know, make her look not quite right somehow."

I looked at Hortense. "Well, my parents like dogs," I said. "We have one. We used to have two, but now we just have this one. We have a baby too, only I don't think he's allergic or anything."

"Oh, well, you could've told by now," Mrs. Jacoby said. "You can tell right away, believe me. The week I got Angela home from the hospital, she was sneezing and she had that terrible rash—do you remember, Frank?—but we never suspected Hortense. For some reason we just never did."

"Angela loved Hortense," Mr. Jacoby said.

"That was the trouble. She'd lie there, letting Hortense lick her all over."

"I guess I should ask my parents," I said.

"Oh, of course," Mr. Jacoby said. "No need to make any final decisions now. Let me give you our phone number and I'll take yours. We can talk the whole thing over at our leisure."

"Should I take her now?" I asked.

"If that wouldn't be too much bother, we'd really appreciate it," he said. "We'll be busy with a lot of things."

"Okay," I said.

I walked across the hall with Hortense and let myself into our apartment. Mom and Dad were in the living room, playing their recorders. Brendan was crawling around the floor. When he saw Hortense, he came rushing over. "Doggie!" he yelled.

"Right, doggie," I said. You have to tell him it's right or he might forget the next time. Sometimes he does anyway. Like he'll call a cat a dog even if they don't look at all alike.

"Hi, Toe," Dad said.

"This is Hortense," I said.

"I figured as much," Mom said. "Aren't you going to bring her back to Mrs. Shorr?"

"Well, I can't," I said. I went into the living room and told them about what happened to Mrs. Shorr.

"Oh, isn't that a shame!" Mom said. "She was such a nice lady."

"Remember how we always used to meet her in the laundry room," Dad said.

I did remember. I used to like it because the laundry room is so dark and gloomy you hate to be down there by yourself, even with Dad. I remember how Mrs. Shorr would get mad if Dad called me Toe because she said Antonia was such a nice name. I guess she must like long names like Hortense.

"I don't see why she died," I burst out suddenly. "All she had was a heart attack."

"People often die of heart attacks," Dad said.

"They do?"

"Yes, it's extremely common."

"But Uncle David didn't. He got better."

"Well, sometimes people get better, especially if they're younger. Their chances of bouncing back are greater."

"I think she'd had a heart attack once before," Mom said. "I think she said that once. That was why she didn't like to overexert herself."

"She was nice," I said.

Dad came over and patted me. "I'm sorry, Toe. I know how much you liked her."

I didn't say anything for a while.

"Who's there now?"

"Her daughter," I said. "Her name is Mrs. Jacoby."

"Oh, yes! She used to live in this building, I remember her. The one with that kind of high-pitched voice?"

"Well, I suppose old Hortense will be happier living out there on Long Island than in the city," Dad said.

"She's not going to," I said.

"Why not?"

"Their daughter's allergic to dogs so they can't take her so I said we would." I spoke really fast.

"Wait just one sec," Dad said. "What did you tell them?"

"I said we'd take Hortense. Please, Dad! Otherwise they might put her to sleep and she's only ten!"

"What makes you think they'll put her to sleep?"

"They might! They might not be able to find a home for her."

"Of course they will," Dad said. "People out on Long Island love dogs."

"But it would be some family she wouldn't even know," I said. "And they might let her loose and she'd get run over." Hortense is very dumb about cars, I know that. Mrs. Shorr always said she was sure she'd get run over if you let her off the leash so I never did the way I do with William sometimes.

"Honey, listen, slow down. We have a dog."

"I know! So how would one more matter? We had two before."

"That was completely different. Elvira was from way back and we got William because we wanted you to have a dog you could grow up with. Hortense is old already."

"She's not so old," I said. "She's ten."

"Well, she's not young. It might be a lot of work looking after her."

"I'll walk her, I'll walk her every time!"

"How can you walk her if you're in school?" Dad said. "Next year Mom and I may both be working."

"But what about William?" I said. "If someone has to walk him, how is it that much more bother to walk Hortense too?"

"It's just an extra thing to worry about. We can't manage it. Dogs eat a lot. If you go away for the weekend, you have to board them some-times, which is expensive. If they get sick—"

"You don't have to give me any allowance for five years," I said.

"Honey, it's not just the money."

"What did you tell them exactly?" Mom said.

"I said I'd ask you."

"Okay, so let's just explain we've talked it over and changed our mind. I'm sure they'll under-stand."

"How can you be so mean?" I said.

Mom and Dad looked at each other. Dad said,

"We can keep her for the weekend, if that'll make it easier for them. But that's it and I mean it. I don't want any more pleading and begging. She's got to go back eventually."

"Okay," I said.

William had come into the room and was sniffing at Hortense. She stood there calmly, the way she usually does.

"What's that thing on her mouth?" Dad said. "Is she vicious?"

I'd forgotten to take off Hortense's muzzle. I bent down and undid it. "No, it's just because she eats . . . well, sometimes she gets hungry and Mrs. Shorr thought she might eat something that wouldn't be good for her, that was poison or something."

"That sounds slightly paranoid," Dad said.

"What does that mean?" I asked.

"Oh just . . . well, it seems a little unlikely anyone would deliberately leave poisoned food around on the street."

"Her digestion may not be so good," Mom said. "Elvira was like that, remember? When she ate grass, she used to throw it up, but she'd go on eating it anyhow."

Hortense eats grass lots of times. I've seen her. She just stands there munching on it, sort of like a cow. Another thing she likes to eat is snow. Just plain snow off the ground. Maybe it tastes like ice cream to her.

Mom and Dad were pretty strong about our not keeping Hortense so I went across the hall to tell Mrs. Jacoby that we could just keep her over the weekend. Mrs. Jacoby said she understood and that she appreciated all I had done for Hortense already. I wonder if she knew Mrs. Shorr used to pay me for walking Hortense. Maybe she thought I did it for free. Actually, maybe I would have done it for free, but since Mrs. Shorr said she would pay me, I said okay.

14

On Sunday an ad will appear in the paper about Hortense in the part about dogs. Mrs. Jacoby asked if we would mind handling the calls.

"She looks kind of dirty, doesn't she?" Mom said. "Maybe we should give her a bath."

William hates having a bath so we hardly ever give him one except on Fire Island where we can hose him off in the yard. But Hortense was more dirty looking, probably because she has these white patches that aren't so white anymore. Also her ears have all this stuff on them from dragging around in the street. I guess it's like a girl with braids would be if she crawled around and her braids dragged on the ground.

"You know what I think the best idea is?" Dad said.

"What?" I kept hoping he would say the best idea was we could keep her.

"Let's put her in the shower. We can use the hose, the one that attaches to the sink."

Actually, that's how Mom used to wash my hair before I learned to do it myself. I would stand in the shower and she would aim this hose at my head and then soap my hair up and rinse it off. What I hate about that hose is that it goes from boiling hot to freezing cold in about three seconds. You can never get it just right.

Dad put Hortense's leash on. She must have thought she was going for a walk because she started wagging her tail like she was happy. I wonder if she knows Mrs. Shorr died. You'd think if she did, she wouldn't be that happy. Sometimes when I come out of the elevator on our floor, she'll sort of stand there like she didn't know which way to turn. Once I even went over and rang Mrs. Shorr's doorbell by mistake. Then all of a sudden I remembered and I felt awful.

Dad led Hortense into the shower stall. There's this part you had to step over to get in and we had to help her because she's slow at moving. Then Dad hooked her leash on one of the faucets.

"Dad, get the water just right," I told him, "or it will be freezing or boiling."

Dad tested the water on himself first and then got Hortense all wet. Then he squeezed some shampoo over her body and began lathering it all over her.

"Can I do that?" I said.

"Sure, go right ahead."

I lathered Hortense everywhere. It was really fun. I had the feeling she liked it too. She stood there, not trying to pull away the way William does. Dad rinsed her off and then said, "Let me work on those ears a minute, will you, Toe?"

He took this nail brush and began brushing the tips of Hortense's ears, which had some dried dirt on them. That was the hardest part, her ears. Then, when all the soap was off, I got this huge bath towel, which we sometimes use at the beach, and we wrapped Hortense up and began rubbing her all over. We didn't get her all dry, just halfway. Then we let her loose.

You should have seen her! She began leaping and jumping around like that picture in *Ferdinand the Bull* where he gets bitten by a bee. "For an old lady, she seems pretty frisky," Dad said.

"Doesn't she look pretty?" I said. Her white parts were really white and her fur was all shiny and nice looking. After she ran around for a while, barking really loudly, she lay down in a patch of sun and went to sleep. I never even knew Hortense *could* bark. I guess she only does it on special occasions.

The next day we did get some calls about her. The ad didn't say how old she was and when we told some people they said that was too old and they didn't want her after all. But one person seemed really interested and said he might call later in the week. Then this lady called and said did we know that we should never advertise an old dog in the paper because someone might buy her for experimental purposes? What the ad said was "mature basset hound" but I guess the lady knew that meant "old." She said she belonged to some society and they like to warn people about what might happen to their dog.

"What did she mean?" I said after the lady hung up. Whenever the phone rings, I let Mom or Dad answer it, but I listen in on the other extension.

"It sounds like an old wives' tale to me," Dad said.

"What kind of experiments did that lady mean?"

"She meant—you know, in a laboratory."

Suddenly I got very scared because one of our teachers once told us how bad it was for people to do that to animals, just kill them for the sake of science. Dad said that was a matter of opinion, that it was one way to find things out about disease and try and find cures. "Anyway, they won't do that to Hortense," he said.

"How do you know?"

"Toe, listen. There are all kinds of weird people in the world with all kinds of weird ideas. You can't go around taking everyone seriously."

"But she didn't sound weird."

"Don't worry. Nothing bad will happen to Hortense."

"But if it did, you wouldn't know. They could just do it and not ever tell you."

Nothing I said seemed to make Dad or Mom care about what happened to Hortense. I don't think it's fair. When Elvira had to be put to sleep, Mom was so sad, and here Hortense might be all chopped up or even worse. When I went with Mom to the butcher store, I saw this picture of a cow, only it was divided up into parts so you could see which part made hamburgers and which part made steaks. It made me think of Hortense because sometimes, especially when she's eating grass, she looks like a cow. I don't know if someone would want to eat her, but you can't tell. Once I was in a store and they had goat meat to buy. Anyway, they could tell people Hortense was a cow.

Hortense was in the butcher store with us, kind of sniffing around like she usually does. There was a cat they always have there and she went over to try and say hello, but the cat scurried away. It's too bad Hortense isn't a cat. Lots of times you see cats in stores and people give them scraps to eat. But you never see a dog. The butcher tossed Hortense a piece of baloney and she gulped it right down, without even chewing it. "You like that, huh?" he said, grinning.

I didn't want to tell him that Hortense eats just about anything. In the days she's been with us, she's eaten celery tops and the parts of carrots that you scrape off. Once Mom was shelling peas and she ate up all the pea pods! And once an egg fell on the floor by mistake and she ate the whole thing, even the shell.

When we got home, it was toward evening. Mom and Dad were supposed to go out, but the baby-sitter called up and said she was sick. I know it isn't nice to say, but I really like it when the baby-sitter gets sick and can't come. Then Mom and Dad can't go out and we can stay home and have pizza and watch TV together. But this time Mom said they had tickets to a play and they just had to go. She began calling all the baby-sitters from this list she keeps in the kitchen on the bulletin board. Finally she came in and said, "Well, Marjorie says she can do it, thank heaven."

Aunt Marjorie is my mother's sister. I really like her. She lives in her own apartment and she sometimes takes me to special shows and movies.

"Who's this?" she said when Hortense ambled over to sniff at her feet. There seems to be something about people's feet that really turns Hortense on. Maybe that's because she's so low to the ground that it's easier for her to smell them. Anyway, she sniffed around and I explained to Aunt Marjorie about Mrs. Shorr and the dog walking and the lady who had called up and said someone might use Hortense for experiments.

"I never heard of that," Aunt Marjorie said. "What kind of experiments?"

"The lady didn't say. She just said it happens all the time and she belongs to this group who go around calling people up." Suddenly I had a terrific idea. "Aunt Marjorie?"

"Umm?" Aunt Marjorie was looking at Brendan, who was still up. He's supposed to go to bed at seven, but Mom was so busy calling baby-sitters that he got behind schedule.

"You could take her," I said.

"Oh no, he's getting the lamp cord!" Aunt Marjorie said.

"It's okay. It's nailed to the wall. So, will you?"

"What? Will I what?"

"Take her."

"Take who? Where? Toe, listen, let's get Brendan in."

"All right. Can't you even talk while you're putting him in?"

"I can't," she said. "Babies make me nervous."

"How come?"

"They just do. I never know what they're going to do next."

I helped Aunt Marjorie change Brendan and get him into his pajamas. Then he stood up and hung on to the crib. "Ooo," he said.

"Does that mean good night?" said Aunt Marjorie.

"Uh-uh. . . . It means he wants us to do the Oodles Boodles dance."

"What in the world is that?"

"I'll show you. Take his hand." Aunt Marjorie took one of Brendan's hands and I took the other. Then I took her hand so we were in a circle. "You don't really dance," I explained. "You just kind of hop around, like you were dancing. And while you're doing it, you sing. You can just pretend to sing."

Aunt Marjorie and Brendan and I all hopped around while I sang the Oodles Boodles song. It is sort of silly, I guess, but you have to do it or else Brendan won't go to sleep. You sing "Oodles boodles, oodles boodles, oodles boodles, oodles boodles" to this special tune.

"Interesting lyrics," Aunt Marjorie said. "Who made them up?"

"I don't know." Brendan was smiling and jumping up and down. "More oo," he said.

"I don't think I can take another round," Aunt Marjorie said.

I went over and turned off the light. "You have to kiss him," I said.

"Any place special?"

"He likes it if you kiss his fingers."

"Wow, this guy has a real routine worked out, doesn't he?" Aunt Marjorie kissed Brendan and I kissed all his fingers and then he lay down. "You do this every single night?" Aunt Marjorie said.

"Well, sometimes Mom or Dad does it. We sort of take turns."

We sat down in the living room. "Do you want to watch TV?" Aunt Marjorie said. "What happened to *Star Trek*? Don't you watch it anymore?"

"It's not on tonight," I said. "Anyway, you said we could talk about what I wanted to."

"I'm sorry, Toe, I don't remember."

I cleared my throat. "About Hortense. Whether you'd take her."

Aunt Marjorie frowned. "Take her where?"

"You know, keep her, like forever, as long as she lives."

"You mean, take her to live with me?"

I nodded.

"Oh, I couldn't, Toe. How could I? You know how small my apartment is."

"She isn't so big," I said. "She's not half as big as a Great Dane."

"No, I know that, but, anyway, it's not just the space, I'm at work all day. How would I look after her?"

"But if you don't, someone will just come and take her and do those things that I said, those experiments!"

"I can see you're upset, Toe, but . . . see, I don't even like dogs that much."

It's hard to imagine someone not liking dogs. "Not even any kind?"

She shook her head. "It's not that I *dis*like them," she said. "I just don't have any special desire for one."

"It could be sort of like your child," I said. "You could pretend. Mom said she used to think of Elvira as her first child."

"That's all I need . . . a pretend child."

"It would be easier than a baby."

"True. But who's talking about babies?"

Hortense had come over and was lying down right next to us, looking up with that sad expression she gets. You could tell she probably knew what we were saying. "Doesn't she look nice?" I said. "We gave her a shower with baby shampoo."

"She looks terrific," Aunt Marjorie admitted.

"She's ten, which is like seventy."

"I hope I look that good at seventy," Aunt Marjorie said.

"And that patch isn't anything bad. It just means you can't show her. Otherwise she could've been a show dog."

Aunt Marjorie put her head to one side. "Toe, I'm afraid you're barking up the wrong tree."

"You just don't want her?"

"I really don't. And a dog should be with someone who loves dogs."

That was true. I think Hortense could tell if Aunt Marjorie just took her and pretended to like her, but really didn't.

When I was lying in bed, I started thinking of everyone I knew who might take Hortense. Then I had another terrific idea—Jimmy! He loves dogs. He told me practically every Christmas and birthday he's ever had he always put a dog down on his list and he never got one. He says he's going to keep on doing it forever and if he never gets one, then as soon as he's grown up and lives by himself, the first thing he'll do is buy a dog.

At school I explained to him about Hortense. I told him how she had this great pedigree and her mother was a famous dog who won ribbons. "She's really friendly, too," I said. "She loves to lick people." Sometimes if Brendan is sitting on the floor, Hortense goes over and licks his whole face. It might be because he's a messy eater and she wants to get the food that's on him. That's what Dad says. But it could also be friendliness.

"Yeah, I'd like to have her," he said, "but I have to ask my parents."

I kept telling him all the good things about Hortense and I explained to him how, if he didn't take her, she would be cut up and used for experiments. He got really worried. He promised he would ask his parents that same night and call me right back.

After supper I was taking a bath when Mom said, "Toe, Jimmy's on the phone. Should I tell him you'll call back?"

"No, let me speak to him," I said. I jumped out of the tub and wrapped this towel around me. I dried my ears but that was all.

"They won't let me," Jimmy said.

"How come?"

"They said she's too old. They said if you get a dog, you should get a puppy so you can train her."

"But she's trained," I said. "She can't do tricks or anything, but she's pretty good about most things. She doesn't get up on chairs."

"Well, that's what they said. So I guess we can't do it."

"Did you tell them she had such a good pedigree?"

"Yeah, only they said so what since they don't want to show her anyway. And they said, Mom said, show dogs are nervous."

"She isn't a show dog!" I said. "It was just her mother. She has that patch."

"Listen, Toe, I want her, but how can I take her if my mom and dad say no?"

That was true. I sighed. It seemed like everyone had some excuse or reason not to take Hortense. Dad said it's the same way about adopting children. The ones that are babies everyone wants, but the older ones nobody will take. They just stay there, sometimes forever, or at least till they're grown up. That doesn't seem fair either.

I guess William will be glad if we don't take Hortense. Whenever she walks into a room, he walks out. It might be because she's a basset hound. He might just not like basset hounds.

Hortense doesn't seem to mind. Or, anyway, even if she does, she just lies there and watches him walk out. She doesn't seem to take it personally. I wonder if she knows she's a basset hound. I also wonder if dogs know they're dogs. I wish someone would find out about things like that, what dogs think about when they lie there so still, just looking around.

15

Today is the day the man from New Jersey is supposed to come and look at Hortense. He's coming after supper. Libby was at school for the first time in around ten days. She had the flu and fever and everything, not just a regular cold. Her temperature was a hundred and five, which is practically as high as it can get.

After school I went with Libby and her mother and Mattie to Baskin-Robbins. Mattie never knows what to pick. She picked pistachio almond twirl just because it was green, I guess, and then she didn't like it. Libby and I had root beer floats. I started telling about Hortense.

"I've always wanted a basset hound," Libby's mother said wistfully, licking Mattie's cone.

I was surprised. "Then how come you didn't ever get one?" Libby said.

"It always seemed so complicated . . . going, picking the right one. And then, when you and Mattie were babies, it would have been hard. But now, maybe the time is ripe."

"Mom, really, can we keep her?" Libby got all

excited. She looked over at me. I felt pretty excited too. "Please Mom, pretty please."

"Libby, cool it, okay? Let's think it over. It's something we have to think about very, very carefully."

"But the man from New Jersey is coming tonight," I said.

"Do you have to let him know right away?"

"I don't know."

"If we got her, you could visit," Libby said. "So it would be almost like you didn't have to give her away!"

"I know." I almost didn't want to think about it because before, when I got excited thinking Aunt Marjorie and Jimmy would take Hortense, it didn't happen. Maybe if I pretend it won't happen this time, it will.

I told Libby's mother that she could even have this book that Mrs. Shorr's daughter gave me called *The Complete Basset Hound,* which told special things about how to take care of them.

"Is she a puppy?" Mattie said.

"A puppy!" Libby yelled. "How can a dog who's ten years old be a puppy? She's practically like a grandmother."

"But she's peppy," I said. I described how we'd washed her and how she jumped around, barking.

"Can she sleep in our room, Mom?" Libby begged.

"Libby, will you calm down? I said we have to think and talk about the whole thing. It's by no means settled."

I went to Libby's house after that and all we could talk about was how great it would be if Libby's mother and father let her keep Hortense. In some ways I felt sort of jealous that Libby would have her, but at least it would be better than if some stranger came and took her and I never saw her again.

"Where would you have her sleep?" I asked.

"I don't know. Maybe in our room."

William sleeps in our kitchen. Mom or Dad closes the door and he can't come out. When you let him out in the morning and give him his breakfast, he starts barking and jumping around.

Libby began telling me how she'd seen this dog bed in a store near our school that just had things for dogs. They have special toys for them made out of rubber to look like bones and special dog coats and even dog boots. "What was the bed like?" I said. We don't have a special bed for William—he just sleeps on an old mat.

"It was really pretty," Libby said. "It had these cushions covered with some kind of material, you know, and it was like a big basket. It really looked comfortable."

"It must be expensive," I said.

"Yeah, probably," Libby said. "But maybe I could save up my allowance and get it."

"I could chip in," I said.

"Oh, sure," Libby said. "You can. Because even if we keep her, it's still sort of like she's yours."

I thought that was nice of Libby to say. "I'd like to visit her."

"You can tell me how to walk her and stuff like that," Libby said. "I never even walked a dog."

"It's not so hard," I said. "Only Hortense sort of yanks you. She's quite strong." I told Libby how sometimes Hortense tries to eat garbage, even with her muzzle on.

"Yuck!" Libby said. "Real garbage?"

"Yeah. But Mrs. Shorr said she never got sick from it. It's just kind of disgusting to watch."

"Maybe she needs more food."

"Uh-uh. Mrs. Shorr said the doctor said bassets can get very fat if you give them all they want to eat. Because they're hunting dogs and if they hunt, they run around a lot, like in the country, but if they don't, they can get fat."

"We have this dog in our building that's really fat," Libby said. "He looks disgusting."

"You can give her snacks," I said, "like pea pods and lettuce . . . but not so much stuff like cookies and candy."

"Would she get cavities if she ate candy?"

"I don't think dogs get cavities so much. Anyway, if they do, they don't have to go to the dentist."

"They're lucky!" Libby said. She has three fillings already in her teeth. I just have one.

That night the man from New Jersey came. Dad was inside, putting Brendan to bed. I could hear him singing the Oodles Boodles song. Mom said, "Won't you sit down?" in that kind of voice grownups use when they're talking together.

The man from New Jersey said his name was Ray Hazelteen. He said he had two basset hounds already and he had a big yard and he would take good care of Hortense. Hortense came over and he petted her and began rubbing her behind the ears. "You look in pretty good shape for an old gal," he said.

Hortense rolled over on her back and let him pat her stomach. You could see all her nipples. She seemed to really like the man.

Dad came out from the bedroom. "Glad to meet you," he said.

"He has two basset hounds," I said.

"Goodness! You must have a lot of space."

"Well, we have ten acres or so. It's a nice bit of land."

"Toe, shouldn't you start getting ready for bed?" Mom said.

The reason I didn't want to do that was I was afraid they might decide to give Hortense to that man without even telling me. After all, it's me who walked her and who knew Mrs. Shorr. So it isn't fair to just give her away without even consulting me. "Mom, could I speak to you a minute?" I said.

Mom went with me into the kitchen. "Look at him, Toe!" she said. "Does that look or sound like a man who would chop Hortense up and do experiments on her?"

"But the lady on the phone said you can't tell. She said those people try to sound nice so you'll give them the dog. They're not dumb! They're not going to just *tell* you."

"Honey, that lady on the phone—I just wish I'd spoken to her. She's gotten you all roiled up about this."

"Anyway, Mom, I told you. Libby's mother said *they* might want her."

"I thought you said that wasn't definite."

"It isn't . . . but if they got her, then I could visit her."

"No, that's true," Mom said. "I didn't know you were so attached to her, Toe."

"Well, I am. Mom, if I go to bed, will you promise not to give her to that man tonight?"

"Okay. I'll tell him we'll think about it."

"Do you swear?"

"Toe, I promised. Isn't that enough?"

I didn't want to say it, but you can't always trust your parents. Lots of times I've told Mom and Dad something and told them not to tell and then they do. Sometimes they say they just forgot or some excuse like that.

I got into bed and tried to listen to what Mom and Dad and the man from New Jersey were saying. But I couldn't so I fell asleep. In the middle of the night I woke up. I jumped out of bed and went into the dining room. That's where Hortense sleeps because Mom and Dad thought she and William might fight if they were together in the kitchen. She was there, under the table, sleeping, but when I came over, she crawled out and began wagging her tail. I was glad Mom didn't break her promise to me.

16

Libby got to keep Hortense. She's had her over a month now. I was going to her house for a sleepover date, but we'd stopped off at that dog store on the way home. Libby's mother said she wouldn't let us buy that special bed. She said it was crazy to spend so much money on a bed for a dog. Libby said she didn't see why we couldn't use our own money that we'd saved up from our allowance and Christmas presents. What's the point of saving if you can't even spend it the way you want? But Libby's mother said the point was to learn how to use money intelligently.

"Anyway," she said, "dogs don't care. They're not like people."

"How do you know?" Libby said. "Just because they can't talk doesn't mean they don't care."

"You've seen her. Hortense is perfectly content with her mat. She's used to it. People get attached to things they're used to."

"I bet *you* wouldn't like it so much if you had to sleep on an old mat," Libby said.

"If I were a basset hound, I might very well," Libby's mother said.

The trouble with arguing about something with a mother is you know they can always have the last word.

"Can we walk her now?" I asked.

"I want to walk my dog," Mattie said.

"Will you quit calling her *your* dog?" Libby said. "If she's anyone's dog, she's mine. Anyway, when you walk her, she yanks you all over the place." Libby let Mattie hold Hortense's leash just while we were in the elevator. Then she took it.

I told her about how a couple with a baby had moved into Mrs. Shorr's old apartment. "They said I could baby-sit for them," I said. "They thought I was older, I guess."

Libby has changed a lot since she got Hortense, I don't know why. She doesn't tease me so much and she's stopped talking so much about being a tomboy. That night, when we were upstairs in our pajamas, we decided to change the name of the club. "Maybe it should be a club just for people who have dogs," Libby said.

"But Ginny and Florence don't *have* dogs," I pointed out.

"So? Then they can't be in it," Libby said.

"Do we *have* to have a club?" I said.

"No, I guess we don't," Libby said. "Anyhow, I don't like Florence so much anymore. All she talks about is horses."

"She said she wanted to *be* a horse," snorting with laughter.

"I know! She's really crazy."

Libby's mother peeked in. "Lib, it's your night for a shower," she said. "You girls can take one together if you like."

"I never took a shower," I said.

"Boy, you must be pretty dirty," Libby said.

"I take baths, dope, not showers." Actually, the reason is I don't so much like the idea of water coming down on my head.

"You can borrow my shower cap, Toe," Libby's mother said.

"But what if water gets in my eyes?" I said.

"So?" Libby said. "That doesn't hurt. It's just like putting your face in the water when you swim."

I don't like doing that so much either.

"I don't like taking baths," Libby said. "You just sit there and the water gets all cold and dirty." She was taking off her clothes. I stared at her. It was really strange. She had breasts! Not really big ones, but she had them.

"When did you get those?" I said. I never even noticed it before.

Libby looked embarrassed. "Don't tell anyone. Promise?"

"Okay. But when did you get them?"

"I don't know. It just seemed like one day I had them."

'pies I " ...?"
."

...t them. I couldn't help it. "Boy,
...ng to have big ones if you started
... Maybe like Mrs. Portel." That's
...cher and hers start at her chin
practica...

Libby looked scared. "Mom says no. She said
it doesn't matter when it starts. Like you could
start growing them early, but then stop early,
too. She said it's hereditary. Hers came early, too."

That made me think about my period. I wondered if I should tell Libby. But in a way it
seemed worse than getting breasts, even.

We got in the shower and Libby turned it on
a good temperature.

"Quit staring at them," she said, handing me
the soap.

"Do you wash them?"

"Of course!"

I couldn't get over it. It seemed so strange. At
least with your period you only get it once a
month or sometimes not so often so you can kind
of forget about it in between time. But breasts
would just be there all the time like a real part
of you.

When we got out, we dried ourselves and got
into our pajamas.

"Do you like having them?" I said. "Or is it,
you know, sort of weird?"

"It's okay," Libby said.

"I guess they're supposed to be pretty," I said.

"I don't see why," Libby said. "I don't think the nipple part is so pretty."

"That's for the baby to drink from. You have to have it."

"I know! Only you can give them bottles too. So you don't *have* to have it."

"You know what I read once in this book?"

"What?"

"Sometimes I take books for teenagers out of the library. I know you're not supposed to, but sometimes they let you. There was this book where this boy sucked on a girl's breasts!"

"Yuck!" Libby said.

"Sometimes I don't know if I want to be a teenager," I said. "You have to do stuff like that." I didn't tell her some of the other things. They were even worse.

"That might've been something they used to do, like a long time ago, but don't anymore," Libby suggested.

"I forget when the book was published," I admitted.

"It might be like some old custom, you know, the way they used to do lots of things they don't anymore."

I hope Libby is right. "If you had a baby," Libby asked, "would you, you know, nurse it?"

"You mean if I had breasts?"

"Well, you're going to get them, idiot! You can't *not* get them."

"I guess I might want to try it," I said. "Mom says it was a great feeling."

"My mother never even did it," Libby said. "She said bottles were easier."

"It seems like they're easier. I guess if nature had known there would be bottles, she wouldn't have invented breasts."

"Maybe after a while they'll go away," Libby said, "like tails."

We were silent, thinking of this.

"That takes hundreds of years, though," I said finally.

"Yeah, I guess it won't help us."

Libby's mother looked in the room. "Girls, did you brush yet?"

"Yes," Libby lied.

"Are you all set, then? Do you want a snack or something?"

"We'll get it ourselves," Libby said. In the kitchen she said, "Let's have cupcakes—but don't let her see."

"Why?"

"She'll make us brush again."

"You didn't brush the first time, even."

"I know. Because sometimes she catches me and says I have to do it twice."

We snuck past Libby's mother, who was reading a story to Mattie. Hortense was spread out on the floor next to them.

"Mattie used to be scared of dogs, but she isn't anymore," Libby said.

"I used to be too," I said. "I mean, Mom says that. I don't remember. It was when I was just a baby."

We got back into bed. I was sleeping on the floor in one of Libby's sleeping bags. Her father had blown up his air mattress and put it under me so I would be more comfortable. They use it for camping. Sometimes when I sleep at someone's house, I can't get to sleep. I could just see the top of Libby's head. She was sleeping on top of the bunk bed.

"Lib?"

"Yeah?"

"Something happened to me that is even worse than getting breasts."

Libby didn't say anything.

"Don't you even want to know what it is?"

"Sure. What is it?"

"I got my period."

Libby sat up in bed. "Oh, come on! You couldn't have. You don't get it till you're twelve or thirteen. Remember—that's what Mrs. Tyroler said in class."

"I know! That's why I was so scared. I was just, like, doing this regular shopping for Mom and Dad at the store and all of a sudden this blood started oozing down my leg."

Libby shuddered.

"I thought maybe it was catsup or something. But then Mom said she got hers early too."

Libby let out a moan. "Oh, no!"

"It's actually not so bad, Lib. Really."

"Doesn't it hurt horribly?"

"Uh-uh. Not at all."

"I don't believe you."

"Really, it doesn't. If you didn't know it was blood, you'd just think it was some stuff coming out of you."

Libby looked suspicious. "So how come Florence said her sister had to be in bed a whole week?"

"I don't know."

"I *hate* blood," Libby said.

"It doesn't seem like blood so much."

Libby was silent a minute. Then she said, "How come you didn't tell me?"

I didn't know if I should say the real reason, that I was afraid everyone in the club would tease me. "I don't know. It just seemed kind of weird, you know, getting it so early."

"You could have a baby!" Libby said, shocked.

"Well, I'm not going to so don't worry."

"Yeah, but just think, you could have one. You better not have Jimmy Sherrill sleep over at your house anymore."

I felt embarrassed. "That's not how you have babies."

"Yes, it is. In that book it said sleeping with someone makes you have babies."

"But you have to be in the same bed," I said. "You have to do all that other stuff."

"I guess." Libby sighed. "Are you *sure* it doesn't hurt, Toe? Do you *swear?*"

"I swear."

"I'm glad you got yours first. That's why I sometimes wish I had an older sister so she could explain what it was like."

"Doesn't your mother ever explain?"

"Oh, sort of. But she was *our* age so long ago."

We didn't say anything for a while. Then I said, "I used to wish I could have puppies."

"You mean, instead of babies?"

"Yeah, they're so cute. And babies always look so wrinkled up and red."

Just then Mattie came in with a book tucked under her arm. Libby's mother walked in behind her. "How are things, girls?" she asked. "Are you okay?"

We nodded.

"Let's not have a lot of whispering and carrying on, all right? I want Mattie to get to sleep."

"*She's* the one who makes all the noise," Libby said, "not us."

Mattie went around gathering up all these dolls to take to bed with her. Some of them were the ones I got her. Her whole bed was covered with them. "These are my babies," she told me.

I remember how I used to sleep with a lot of stuffed animals when I was little, but I don't so much anymore. Just sometimes I'll take my Snoopy and the raccoon pillow, but that's all.

"I guess we better not talk about—you know, anymore," Libby said.

"Okay," I said.

"What's you know?" said Mattie.

"Something you wouldn't understand," Libby said.

"I would too!"

"How do you know? You don't even know what it *is*!"

"I'll get Mommy and she'll make you tell me," Mattie said.

"It's nothing special, Mattie," I said. "We were just talking about Hortense."

"I understand about her!" Mattie said indignantly.

"Libby was just teasing," I said.

We lay there while Mattie sang to herself for a while. Then finally I could hear her breathing slowly. "Lib?"

"Yeah?"

"I think she fell asleep."

"Good. Toe, I was just thinking."

— 114 —

"What about?"

"Well, my birthday. Maybe I'll have boys this year."

"Which ones?"

"Just the nice ones, not all of them."

"Not Leo or Max," I said.

"Are you kidding? Of course not *them*!"

"Jimmy could come. . . ."

"Yeah, and maybe Harry and Chris."

"You won't play those games with kissing or anything, will you?" I said, suddenly uneasy.

"Of course not! It'll just be, like, a regular party."

We were quiet again for a while. Then I said, "Lib, will you promise something?"

"What?"

"To not tell anyone about—you know—my period and all that."

"Okay," Libby said. "Don't you tell anyone about my breasts either."

"I won't." But I thought that sooner or later people would notice. I didn't say that to Libby, though.

Libby fell asleep before me. I could tell because she makes this sort of snoring sound when she sleeps. Not real snoring, but a little like it. I lay in bed, and while I was trying to go to sleep myself, Hortense came into the room. She sniffed around and finally settled down in the corner.

I'm glad Libby got to keep her. I think Mrs. Shorr would rather have it that way than if Hortense was with a complete stranger. I think if she knew about it, she'd be glad.

NORMA KLEIN'S reputation for perceptive and honest explorations of youngsters' worlds has grown ever since the publication of her first celebrated book for children, *Mom, the Wolfman, and Me.* She is the author of more than 20 books for children, young adults, and adults, including *Confessions of an Only Child, Naomi in the Middle,* and the recent title *No More Saturday Nights.*

Ms. Klein is a graduate of Barnard College and holds an M.A. degree in Slavic languages from Columbia University. She lives with her husband in New York City.

Meet Antonia Henderson in her first book,

Confessions of an Only Child . . .

"I've always liked being an only child. But my parents decided they really wanted another baby, so I guess I'm in for it now. My friend Libby has a baby sister who's nothing but a pest, and she stinks, too! Dad keeps telling me I'll get used to the new baby, and that I'll get to teach it everything I know, like how to talk and stuff. Maybe. I just hope it grows up into a nice person. Like me."

"Hurray for Norma Klein! Her writing is honest, funny and intelligent as she deals with real feelings and contemporary relationships."
—*The San Francisco Chronicle*

A Bullseye Book published by Alfred A. Knopf, Inc.